A
Harlequin
Romance

D1462639

Irene had given Guy up because she felt obliged to take care of me. She said she could see you and Irene were sweet on each other, really, but that the very same thing would happen. That I was a burden.'

Past crying, she looked up at him piteously, and very gently he stroked her cheek.

'I can tell you one thing. I love Irene and want to marry her – and have you with us always. And your granny, too. But do you think Irene would ever like me enough to marry me?'

'I know she would, though I can't exactly explain why. So does Granny. But, Uncle David, married couples like to be alone together—'

'Not in Cyprus. They're quick off the mark having babies, and a big girl like you could be no end of a help.'

She smiled then, gave a great sigh, and in the flutter of an eyelid was asleep.

Down in the sitting-room Mrs. Vassilou gave him a penetrating glance, then smiled.

'It's very unconventional at this hour, but I'm leaving you two to talk – for five minutes, no more.'

David grinned at her. 'My watch has a second hand. I promise to clear out on the dot.'

'Good. I'm dropping. And tomorrow I shall have Delphine and Andreas on the doorstep, explaining why they've behaved like a couple of proud, blind, obstinate *donkeys* all these years! Silly young fools!'

When they were alone David went across to Irene and drew her into his arms.

'I've known, ever since that day at Bella Pais, that you were the one woman in the world for me – though I've been stupid enough to fight against it. Could you come to love me a little? Josie thinks you might.'

She shook her head, a glint of laughter in her eyes.

'Not a hope! Because I already love you so very, very much!' And as he held her closely, her head against his shoulder, she went on, giggling weakly: 'You said you'd as soon kiss a tiger!'

'We've both said a heap of crazy things. Now we'll wipe the slate and start again. Oh, there's one condition attaching to our marriage!'

'You haven't asked me to marry you yet.'

'I'm doing so now. But you must promise that Josie will belong to me as well as to you.'

'You really want her?'

'I do. And oh, my darling, how I want you – ache for you.'

Her answer was to raise her soft, parted lips to his, to cling to him.

Until the sound of a thump from the Kyria's ebony stick on the floor of her bedroom made them spring apart, and Irene, exhausted but overflowing with happiness, went running up to bed.

To her relief Josie was fast asleep, but there was the trace of a smile on her face, echoing the smile of the Lady and the Babe in the dim light of the icon.

GOOD NEWS
for HARLEQUIN FANS!

WE'RE REALLY EXCITED . . .
and hope you will be too!

We've finally been able to come up with reprints of forty-eight of some of the very first HARLEQUIN ROMANCES!

Written by such popular authoresses as Rosalind Brett, Essie Summers, Elizabeth Hoy, etc., these new "OLD" books have been in tremendous demand, and we're very pleased indeed to be able to offer them to you. Check the back of this page for the assortment available.

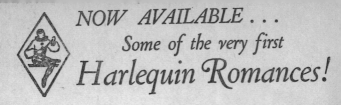

NOW AVAILABLE . . .
Some of the very first
Harlequin Romances!

ORANGE BLOSSOM ISLAND

by

JULIET ARMSTRONG

HARLEQUIN BOOKS

TORONTO   •   WINNIPEG

First published in 1970 by Mills & Boon Limited,
17 - 19 Foley Street, London, England

SBN 373-01493-7

© Juliet Armstrong 1970

Harlequin Canadian edition published May, 1971
Harlequin U.S. edition published August, 1971

Printed in Canada

For
CHARLES AND MARY
with love

Nicosia 1969

CHAPTER ONE

MOVING restlessly in her chair in a corner of the airport lounge, Irene Meredith thought she had never known so long a night.

Would morning never come? And even if it did at last, would it bring any firm confirmation of the delayed flight to Cyprus?

True, a message had boomed over the loudspeaker more than once, indicating hopes that the weather over the Mediterranean was improving, that the unseasonable falls of snow were lessening. But she was too tired for optimism, and far too tired for sleep.

She glanced at nine-year-old Josie, close beside her, and envied her capacity for drifting so easily into a deep slumber. How sweet and serene she looked, snuggled up like that, curling dark lashes etched against her cheek, dark, shining curls rumpled.

But Josie, very naturally, had experienced nothing of the fatigue and anxiety which her elder sister had undergone during recent months. *Her* worst ordeal had been trying, without much success, to conceal from Aunt Ethel's sharp eyes her delight at the prospect of leaving her – of going with Irene to Cyprus to live with this unknown grandmother of whose affection and kindliness she had heard so much.

She was blissfully ignorant of the grave warnings that Mr. Blake, the family solicitor, had given Irene of the danger of tearing up roots, of spending her small capital, inherited so recently on her twenty-first birthday, on what might well prove a disastrous course. Had only received – and that with cultivated stoicism – the backlash of Aunt Ethel's bitter comments to Irene on the folly and ingratitude of cutting adrift from herself and Uncle Herbert after all the generosity and kindness shown them since their parents' death, five years ago.

There had been that one dreadful little scene, of course, when Uncle Herbert had put down his newspaper and, looking over his spectacles, had interrupted Aunt Ethel's nagging by saying – curtly, for him – 'My dear Ethel, don't be a humbug. If anything, we've been grossly overpaid, by the terms of my brother's will, for anything we've done for my nieces.'

An observation which had so enraged Aunt Ethel that Irene had had to bundle the child out of the stuffy little sitting-room before a violent tirade began concerning the heavy expenses which he seemed to ignore and the continual worry which the girls had caused by their selfish and secretive behaviour.

Always adept at finding the wounding remark, Aunt Ethel had lately produced a fresh barb by references to 'that fellow Guy Cosway', the man whom Irene had been expecting to marry but whom, since Christmas, she had never mentioned. References to the vanity and stupidity of girls who set their cap at rich men – sons of their employers, no less! – imagining them to have serious intentions.

Bland silence had been the only possible answer to such taunts because, for very different reasons, neither Aunt Ethel nor Josie must be allowed to have the least idea why the 'understanding' had ended. Which was, in fact, because Guy had refused point-blank to have Josie living with them after he and Irene were married.

He had put it down to his great love for Irene. He wanted his wife to himself – wanted her to be carefree and happy, not burdened with a nine-year-old girl. The child could perfectly well, he maintained, stay on with her aunt and uncle. Or, if Irene preferred, he would gladly pay her fees at a first-class boarding-school. See that she was sent off for decent holidays – coming to them for the odd week-end, of course.

She didn't blame him for his attitude. At twenty-six he couldn't understand how the shock of her parents' death in a plane accident, followed by five years with an aunt who frankly disliked her, had made the child cling to her elder sister.

'But, Guy, I've always told her,' she had explained in distress, 'that when I reached my twenty-first birthday, and was given the guardianship of her under our father's will, we'd leave Aunt Ethel, and have a home together.'

'Then you shouldn't have done it,' had been his angry response. 'A girl of twenty-one tied up to a kid sister! It's crazy, and if you really cared for me you'd admit it – and look for a sensible solution.'

Tears stung her eyes now, as she thought of Guy – how sweet and loving he had been before the question of marriage and all that it entailed had come up. Of his unhappy, angry, *incredulous* expression when she had insisted that she could not give way over Josie.

As though her painful thoughts had somehow communicated themselves to her, the child shifted in her chair and waking up looked at Irene anxiously.

'I'm hungry, Irene. Is it nearly morning?'

'Not yet, darling. And don't talk too loud. Some of the people are asleep.'

'Are you comfy?'

'Not very, Josie. What about you?'

'I'm fine. Only I do wish I could have a nice hot drink.'

'So you shall when morning comes. Everything's closed down now.'

The little girl gave a deep sigh.

'I think it was mean of Aunt Ethel not to let us have a thermos when you found yours was broken. She's got two. No, three, with the grand one she won in that competition.'

'Never mind. Aunt Ethel can't help being the way she is. Here's some barley sugar.' Now that they had escaped, she could speak more charitably of their aunt.

'I've a better idea than that!' A quiet, masculine voice, speaking with a faintly foreign accent, made them look up sharply, and there was a tall, dark young man standing in front of them, holding a thermos jug. 'There's some

9

perfectly good soup left here. I filled up before the restaurant closed. You're more than welcome to it. Tomato soup!'

Josie sat up very straight, and beamed at him: a thin, rather pale little girl.

'Tomato's my favourite. Irene likes it, too.'

'That's good.' He smiled at Irene. 'I'm afraid you'll have to share a cup.' And then he added, still looking at Irene: 'I've a travelling rug I'm not using, if you'd care to borrow it.'

His manner was so gentle, so courteous, that Irene had no hesitation in accepting the offer of soup, though declaring that she did not at all need the rug. And when Josie pressed him to come and sit near them, she found herself supporting the invitation by a smile.

Both girls felt better after the hot drink, but though Josie dropped asleep again almost at once, Irene, still tired and strung-up, remained wakeful.

'If you aren't going to sleep, may I continue to sit with you for a while?' the young man asked.

'As you please!'

'Well, it's rather eerie sitting alone, surrounded by silent or, occasionally, snoring people. It's like some modern, symbolical picture, portraying people waiting for the day of judgment.'

A shadow crossed her face at that.

'A little too close to truth, don't you think! Oh, I know that plane accidents are very rare nowadays, considering the enormous amount of traffic. But our parents died in a crash near Cyprus five years ago.'

'I'm terribly sorry to have been clumsy. But I'm glad you're going to Cyprus, not just to Athens, like so many of these travellers. I shall be living in Nicosia. Andreas Nikolaides is my name.' And he pulled out a little visiting card.

She took it from him politely, and slipped it into her handbag. Not that she was at all likely to refer to it, she thought. But one certainly couldn't snub such a kind and courteous person.

'We're going farther north,' she told him. 'In the Kyrenia direction.'

'You couldn't have a better place for a holiday. And you'll find lots of English people there. No difficulty with language. Not that there would have been much trouble with that. Most of us speak some English, anyway.'

'You yourself speak it almost perfectly.'

'I had much of my training in England.' And he added, smiling: 'Do you know any Greek? I suppose not!'

She hesitated. Ought she to talk freely to this strange young man? Yet why not? She had nothing to tell him that all the world might not hear.

So she said evenly: 'Until I was sixteen – which was five years ago – I spoke Greek as fluently as English. You see, our mother was a Greek Cypriot! Our father, who was English, had a job in Cyprus – that's how he met Mother – and I lived with them in Larnaca until I was thirteen. Then his firm moved him back to England.' She broke off, embarrassed. 'But I must be boring you with all this.'

'Not in the very least! Please go on.' His dark eyes were serious, and very sympathetic.

'There isn't much more to say – about the past, anyway. Since we lost our parents we've been living with relatives in England. Now we're coming to stay with our grandmother, who owns and runs a hotel a few miles along the coast from Kyrenia. The Hermes, it's called.'

Those dark eyes of his opened very wide at that.

'So you're Kyria Vassilou's granddaughters – you and the little girl. I can see now that you both have a certain look of her, in colouring and feature, but your eyes are different. If you won't think me too personal, they're the clear, bright blue of our Cyprus pimpernels.' And before she could make a dry reference to his literally 'flowery compliments' or, more important, to his apparent acquaintanceship with her grandmother, he went on with a smile: 'At first glance, from where I was sitting, I thought you were a young mother with her little daughter. But when I came closer, even before I heard the child use your Christian name, I saw that it couldn't possibly be so.'

'I've mothered Josie so much that I'm near forgetting, sometimes, that I'm her elder sister. It was utterly bewildering for her, the sudden loss of an adoring mama. And the aunt we've been living with happens not to be the maternal type at all. Finds children nothing but a nuisance, and can't help showing it. Because of this, Josie has clung to me much more than she would otherwise have done.'

'Children are cherished in Cyprus. Kyria Vassilou will love her.'

Irene's face brightened.

'I'm sure she will. She was sweet to me when I was a child.' And then she asked: 'Do you know her at all?'

'Not really. My parents – they're dead now – stayed at the Hermes sometimes when they were living in Nicosia. I, too. But not for a long while. And things have changed there, I hear, since she took on a manager. I gather that this chap's mother is Cypriot – a distant connection, by marriage, of the Vassilou family – and his father a dour Scot. And that he takes after his father. Doesn't always see eye to eye with your grandmother.'

For the first time Irene felt more than a tremor of doubt over her wisdom in accepting the rather vague invitation which had come from her grandmother on this all-important twenty-first birthday – to bring Josie over and settle in Cyprus, helping at the family hotel.

She had pointed out in a letter to her grandmother that she had had no training whatever in hotel management – only in secretarial work. That her one other asset was a gift for foreign languages, which her parents had always encouraged, letting her take part in exchange student schemes. It was this rather unusual proficiency which had helped her to obtain a good post in a London shipping office. Apart from Greek, she was fluent in French and German and had a slight knowledge of Swedish.

She added that she was interested in good food and in

home-making, but had had almost no chance of practising these arts!

Mrs. Vassilou, who spoke English better than she wrote it, had cabled a one-word reply: 'Come.' And here she was, hearing for the first time that her grandmother, who for some time had been alone at the helm of the Hermes, now employed a manager; a man who sounded as though he might prove difficult to work for.

'Don't look worried,' Andreas said, mildly surprised at the way her attractive face had clouded. 'Why should you care what David MacLeod is like? It's your grandmother who matters, surely. She's a character, but everyone likes her. And no doubt she's longing to see you.'

'I remember her as warm and loving,' she said. 'Josie, of course, has no recollection of her at all. She's just stolidly certain that no one could be so unlikeable as the Aunt Ethel we're leaving.'

'What was so bad about Aunt Ethel?' he asked lazily.

'In the first place, she couldn't bear our mother – labelled her "a foreigner", as though that was the only important thing about her. But then she's a compulsive labeller. Children are invariably "brats", for instance, and people of better education than herself, "damned snobs".'

'Why did your uncle marry her?'

'I suppose she was pretty, in a way, when she was young. Perhaps disillusionment was mutual. He's sweet, but ineffective, Uncle Herbert – or he'd have stood up for us more often: stopped her subtle bullying.'

And then, breaking into their rather odd conversation – just as she had begun to wonder how on earth she came to be discussing her relatives with a complete stranger – the longed-for announcement came booming through the lounge that the weather over the Mediterranean was clearing rapidly, and that passengers for Athens and Cyprus should prepare to join their plane.

It was a relief to Irene that Andreas Nikolaides continued to take her and Josie under his wing. Self-reliant as she had learned to be, her weariness of mind and body made her unashamedly thankful for a male escort, especially one who knew the ropes so well.

They stuck to him, going up into the plane, and at once he manoeuvred things so that the three of them sat together – Irene in the middle, and Josie by the window so that if she woke up early she could peep out – even if there was nothing more than an expanse of cotton-wool cloud to be seen.

Once settled in her seat, with Andreas' travelling rug to provide extra comfort, sleep came at last to Irene, as to most of her fellow-passengers, and she dreamed more peacefully than for many weeks. Dreamed that Guy had slipped back into her life, with all his old sweetness, his protective care for her; that they were planning the home which Josie would, quite naturally, be sharing with them.

It was painful to wake up to reality, but Josie's happy excitement at seeing land far below, and Andreas' smiling good-morning, forced her to shake off sadness and pretend, at least, to enter into their cheerful mood.

The arrival of breakfast helped. It had always been a pretty dismal meal in Maida Vale, with Aunt Ethel presiding at the tea-pot and complaining non-stop about rising prices, while Uncle Herbert hid behind his newspaper. But this was very different.

The little trays handed out now were most inviting. And it was fun to hear Josie's delighted exclamations as she observed and investigated the contents of the neat little envelopes containing plastic cutlery, sugar, powdered milk, or what have you!

Rather to her surprise – for she had had little appetite of late – she found herself as hungry as Josie and Andreas, who quickly cleared their trays. Feeling far better, too, and more hopeful of turning her back firmly on the unhappy past, and looking forward steadily to the future – the shadowy figure of 'dour' David MacLeod notwithstanding.

She had not intended to talk to Andreas any more about her affairs. It was time she encouraged him to speak about himself. But after explaining that he was a chartered accountant who, after taking a course in the North of England and working there for some years, was now returning to join a firm in Nicosia, he asked her how long she would be holidaying in Cyprus – for he would like to take her and Josie for a drive – if her grandmother could spare them for an afternoon.

'We won't be holidaying, Mr. Nikolaides!' Josie was bending round to look at him. 'We're going to our grandmother for keeps. I'll be going to school, and Irene will be helping in the hotel.'

For a moment Andreas looked astonished and faintly embarrassed. But recovering himself quickly, he observed pleasantly that this was good news, as it would give him the chance, he hoped, of seeing more of them.

But presently, when Josie was absorbed in trying to get a good view of the Greek islands, far below, he murmured to Irene: 'Don't take any notice of what I said about Kyria Vassilou's manager. He's certain to give his employer's granddaughter top treatment. However, if, by any remote chance, he did make you unhappy – played you up! – don't forget that you've a friend in me, and in my relations, too, I'm sure.'

Remembering the kindness and affection which she had received from her grandparents in past years – her grandfather had been alive then – Irene could not believe she had much cause for apprehension. All the same, it was good to feel that she had friends – potential friends, anyway – outside the hotel and its occupants.

Her mood changed presently, however. Stupid though it might be, she was feeling oddly nervous when, after a brief stop at Athens, the plane eventually crossed the coastline of Cyprus, and came in to land at the Nicosia airport. Had she, after all, been a fool to give up her well-paid post in London and come to work for her grandmother who had not so much as mentioned pocket-money? Had she – this an even more vital question – broken too impulsively with Guy? Failed him by not trying hard enough to understand his attitude? By not playing for time, and patiently seeking a compromise solution?

But Josie's hand clutching hers, the child's half-scared delight over what she termed 'our adventure', helped Irene to shrug off last-minute fears. She was smiling with every appearance of serenity as she said good-bye to Andreas and, escorted through the Customs by the friendly porter he had found for her, went in search of her grandmother's car.

However, it was a man who came forward to greet them – a broad-shouldered man in jeans, with an almost imperceptible limp, who gave them a somewhat casual welcome, and apologized shortly for his appearance by a reference to a spot of trouble with the new kitchen range.

'Mrs. Vassilou would have been here to meet you herself,' he went on, ushering them into a large estate car. 'But she's threatened with a migraine.'

'She still has them, poor darling?' Irene's memory had given her a little jolt.

The big man – he was brown-haired, with steady grey eyes – observant eyes, she guessed – nodded.

'But not so often as she used. They don't last so long, either. She got worried about the delay to your plane. Wouldn't be convinced that there'd been no accident. That's been the trouble this time.'

There was room for the three of them to sit in the front of the car – 'Just as we sat in the plane with Mr. Nikolaides,' Josie proclaimed in her high childish voice. Then, as the car loaded, they started on their way, she continued joyfully: 'We thought it would be cold here, from all they said at the airport about snow-storms, but it's hot and dry and lovely.' And cuddling up against Irene she added as a final note: 'Isn't it super to think we're really here? Two thousand, three hundred miles from Aunt Ethel. That's what Mr. Nikolaides said.'

'Doesn't he like your Aunt Ethel either?' Evidently this manager fellow was not always grim. His tone was amused.

'He wouldn't if he knew her. Most people don't. My friends at school said she positively froze them. Mr. Nikolaides wouldn't be scared, of course. But anyway, we only met him last night in the airport lounge. He shared his soup with us. Tomato soup it was. We were *starving*!'

'You'll have plenty to eat at the Hermes,' he assured her. 'What your grandmother hasn't planned in the way of meals for this holiday of yours—' He broke off to introduce himself. 'Your names I know. Mine is David MacLeod. And I'm your grandmother's manager – or if I'm specially in favour, her junior partner.'

'That sounds a little odd!' was Irene's comment.

He gave a slightly satirical smile.

'Oh, she's a wonderful person, but she has her moods.'

'Aunt Ethel had moods,' Josie told him disconsolately. 'Especially when she wasn't having luck with her competitions. I hope Granny won't get cross with me the way she did.'

'Lay off Aunt Ethel, darling,' Irene urged her. And David MacLeod told the child reassuringly: 'Don't you worry. Your grandmother is just set to spoil you disgracefully. In fact, when you get back to this aunt of yours—'

'But we're never going back to Aunt Ethel,' Josie expostulated. 'We're going to *live* with Granny.'

He glanced across at Irene in evident surprise.

'Are you? That's news to me.' But then, plainly determined to pursue the matter no farther, he went on lightly: 'Tell me, both of you, have you ever seen anything so lovely as these masses of yellow daisies at the roadsides— these marvellous wattle trees?'

'Sheer gold,' Irene murmured, but the praise, though apt, was mechanical. Those fears on her arrival at Nicosia airport had taken hold of her again with added force.

It was extraordinary that their grandmother shouldn't have told her manager – junior partner, or whatever he was – that she and Josie were coming permanently to the Hermes.

Could it possibly be that the old lady, whom she had not, after all, seen for eight years, had become a shade senile – hadn't, in spite of her letter and cable, expected her to take seriously the offer of a permanent home?

If so, what in the name of wonder would be her next step – her job in England thrown up – her tiny capital, apart from the sum set aside for Josie's maintenance and education, frittered away on the expenses of this mad adventure?

She found it hard to chat now, but mercifully Josie had plenty to say for herself. Regardless of her two grown-up companions' near-silence, she carried on an excited monologue, exclaiming with wonder at one unfamiliar sight after another – the herdsmen tending their small, mixed flocks of sheep and goats, the little stone houses, the fields full of wild flowers of every colour.

They passed, presently, through the outskirts of Nicosia – city of white buildings and flowering shrubs – 'where our friend Mr. Nikolaides lives,' Josie announced importantly – and took the road to Kyrenia, the lovely highway, dotted with Turkish hamlets, which, Irene recalled now, she had travelled many a time in the past with her parents.

'You've been along here before, Josie,' she told her little sister. 'I remember Mother holding you in her lap, singing a little Greek folk-song to you, while I was pretending to help our father drive the car by making hand-signals. It was hot, and you were very sleepy.'

'Sing the song now,' Josie pressed her. Before she could answer, David had glanced at her in surprise. 'Isn't that rather a tall order? After all these years in England!'

She smiled.

'I could sing it, but I'm not going to this minute. There's too much I want to look at. Josie must wait – and then perhaps I'll teach it to her.'

Indeed beauty surrounded them as they went on their way in the Cyprus spring. By the verges there were still those massed yellow daisies and oxalis, fringing the fields with burnished gold – fields in which, these early days of April, short green corn was already in ear, ready, David remarked, to be harvested in a few weeks.

Birds, too, she remembered, pointing out to Josie – almost a child herself, for the moment – the tiny black and white 'chats', as common in this region as sparrows in London.

When the road left the wide plain for the foothills of the Kyrenia Range, and began to climb into the mountains, the aspect of the countryside changed. In the valleys orchards of karobs and olives still flourished, with here and there a Judas tree flaunting its purple splendour, and guava bushes, red as fire. And on the hillsides those small herds of sheep and goats – a few cows, even – found pasture. But as they made their twisting way higher, conifers replaced most of the deciduous trees, and the scenery became grander – awe-inspiring, even. Yet there was nothing gloomy about it.

Perched crazily on the mountain peaks were those famous old Crusader castles – yes, and there were the rosy ruins of Bella Pais, the Gothic abbey which still, even in its shattered state, kept the peaceful atmosphere of bygone monastic days. Where, in the ancient chapel, villagers still gathered for worship. Nearer at hand little streams of silver fell tumbling down through great grey rocks. Patches of grass still gave grazing for the more agile animals. And there were stretches of cyclamen and of cistus, too, covering the ground as though with delicately coloured embroidery.

Josie clamoured to get out to explore this exciting new world, to pick the tiny flowers, but David was firm in his insistence that any further delay in their arrival would worry their grandmother. There would be plenty of time later on for getting around, he consoled her, adding that some day, if he could find the time, he would bring her and her sister up here for a picnic.

His voice was brusque, but Irene found herself wondering whether he was as tough as Andreas had implied. True, he was far from handsome, in comparison with Andreas himself, or with Guy. But there was character in his rugged features, and in his penetrating grey eyes. Strength in his broad shoulders.

Manners? He seemed reasonably considerate. But charm was a quality which seemed to have passed him by. Maybe she was prejudiced. Even Andreas' compliments and little acts of courtesy lacked spontaneity when set against Guy's attractions, his adorable, adoring ways.

Guy! Why must he keep forcing his way into her mind? It was sheer weakness on her part. Must she forever be comparing him with the other men she met!

Her thoughts were deflected by the view which suddenly met her eyes at the summit of the switchback road. There ahead lay the sea, shimmering in sunlight – a stretch of midnight blue water, streaked with the vivid tints of a kingfisher in flight. Utterly beautiful!

'Oh, darling!' She was hugging Josie in her excitement. 'That glorious view. It's never the same, however often you see it. And the white towers!'

'It's lovely. But when can I go bathing?' Josie's eyes shone.

David glanced down at her, smiling. 'All in good time!' And to Irene he said: 'I don't think you'll find Kyrenia changed much. I've lived in the district five years now, and still regard it as one of the most beautiful places I've ever seen. Which is saying quite a lot!'

'You've travelled widely?'

He nodded. 'I was in the British Merchant Navy until I had an accident to my foot and took this job with your grandmother. The Vassilous are related to my mother's family, you know, and my parents live out here – in the south of the island.'

'Was it a bad accident?' Josie demanded sympathetically. 'Awful sharks going for you, or something like that?'

'Oh, no! Nothing at all exciting! Don't let's talk of

boring things when there's so much to see.'

His voice was brusque, and Josie, easily chilled, said no more – quickly distracted, anyway, by the scene before her.

As they drove slowly into the little town, Irene agreed with David's warm appreciation of it: the absence of change. There was the lovely harbour, flanked by its ancient stone walls and castle, the gaily coloured boats, reflected in the water, the fisher girls drying rose and primrose nets in the sunshine, talking and laughing as they worked. How good it would be to walk here again on the quayside and along the cobbled steets, recalling this and that building – even, perhaps, encountering people known in her childhood.

'We mustn't stop now. You'll have plenty of time for exploring,' David told them, his voice firm, but no longer edgy. 'I'll give you just a minute to look far across the sea. Can you spot a soft grey line, Josie? Irene will have seen it many times.'

'I can see it. I thought it was a low cloud,' the child told him. 'Oh, and I can see much higher white clouds behind.'

'Clever girl! Well, you're looking at the coast of Turkey, forty miles away, and the snow-capped Taurus Mountains.'

Josie whistled through her teeth in a way which Aunt Ethel had never permitted.

'It's like a fairy-tale,' she said.

They passed through the old town, with its white walls and flowering shrubs, its half-hidden gardens, and turning east along the coast road came, after a few miles, to the Hermes Hotel, standing proudly in its sunlit grounds, overlooking the sea.

And now, to Irene's surprise, the sense of recognition failed her. This was not the rambling old house that she remembered with such affection, but something bigger and far more imposing.

She said as much to David, and he smiled

confidently.

'Your grandmother and I have done a lot in the past five years,' he said. 'The old place was very attractive, but it had become vital to move with the times. The modern tourist, on whom the economy of the island is beginning to depend more and more, demands increasing amenities. Suites with private bathrooms, for instance, are no longer regarded as luxuries. We're often asked for them. Could do with more than we have.'

'I'm sad, all the same, that the old place has changed. I loved it so much.'

'Oh, we haven't pulled it down. When we started rebuilding we took care to incorporate the rooms which your grandmother has always occupied into a small, separate wing, keeping the old front of this part intact, so far as we could.'

'That was imaginative of you!'

'I'm afraid I had other ideas. But she's a very determined person, Kyria Vassilou.'

She gave him a brief, considering glance, but now, driving through the grounds, he was pointing out to Josie, wide-eyed with surprise, orange blossom and fruit growing together on the trees; lemons flourishing in the same way.

And then, on the steps of the old white house which Irene remembered now as though it was yesterday, stood her grandmother in the very same sort of long black silk dress she had always worn, a black chiffon scarf veiling her silver hair. She was beautiful still in face and figure, despite a few more lines, and a slight stoop, and she was smiling happily, bright dark eyes alight with pleasure, as she called out in Greek a loving welcome, and opened her arms to them.

Irene ran up the low steps and hugged her, then brought Josie forward. The child, lifting her face for her grandmother's kiss, was shy at first, but managed after a moment to produce the polite Greek version of 'Good morning' which Irene had taught her way back in Maida Vale, when there was not much hope of ever coming to

22

Cyprus. '*Kalimera Sas!*'

The old lady laughed and patted her cheek. 'Clever girl,' she said in correct but halting English. 'We must give each other language lessons, you and I.'

'But you know much more English, Granny, than I know Greek.' Josie was smiling up at her now.

'My dear, I had to learn so that I could talk to my English clients,' her grandmother told her pleasantly. 'But my tongue is still stiff.'

'I'm much worse off than that. Irene tried to teach me, but Aunt Ethel got so cross—'

'The child seems to have got this Aunt Ethel of hers on the brain.' It was David who broke in, frowning, as he brought their suitcases along. And he added, with rather an odd look at Mrs. Vassilou: 'Says she's never going back to her ever. That she's staying here for good.'

'So?' The old lady's voice was bland. But to the girls she said, as though David had made no remark at all: 'Come along, my dears. Irene, I've put you both into the nice room you usually slept in when your dear parents, God rest their souls' – she crossed herself devoutly – 'brought you here.'

Although this wing was now regarded, it seemed, as old-fashioned, the first-floor room into which she led them was large and very lofty by English standards, its size emphasized by white-painted walls and woodwork. French windows opened on to the stone balcony and Irene, running out, declared that there was still the same orange tree, breaking into blossom, and trying to spread into the room. Then, coming back, noted with delight the same icon, of the Virgin and Child, in its old place on the wall.

'But you will find the hotel proper different in many ways,' her grandmother told her – and surely there was a faint tinge of regret in her voice. 'David MacLeod, my very efficient manager – a distant cousin of my dear husband on his mother's side, but far more of a Scot by temperament – has the necessary up-to-date ideas. I find him invaluable. Only occasionally do we differ.'

Irene cocked an eyebrow at her.

'And what happens then? He has a pretty obstinate chin.'

Mrs. Vassilou shrugged her shoulders, faintly amused at the question. But her reply was non-committal. 'Sometimes one thing, sometimes another. I, too, can be stubborn.'

Down in the dining-room, the walls of which were decorated with family photographs of all ages and sizes, variously framed, the three of them sat down to lunch. Lamb *kleptico* was the first dish served – made still more delicious to Josie by her grandmother's explanation that it was cooked, as nearly as possible, in the way that robbers in olden times cooked stolen sheep in earthen ovens, hidden away in the countryside.

'You know about kleptomania,' Irene put in, and Josie nodded vigorously. 'Of course. What Aunt Ethel says is a bare-faced excuse for pinching from the self-service store.'

The child's references to Aunt Ethel – far more frequent since they had left her – troubled Irene. She came to the conclusion that Josie, for all her apparent gaiety, was suffering from a subconscious fear that this new life which was opening out for them in Cyprus was too good to be true, that the links between her aunt and herself might not really have snapped for all time. It made her more eager than ever to find out for certain if the old lady had meant her to take her invitation in earnest.

The opportunity came quickly. Lunch over, Mrs. Vassilou decreed gently that Josie should go upstairs for a brief siesta, while Irene stayed downstairs for a chat.

Sitting together over coffee, Irene soon learned that she need have no fears for the future. Mrs. Vassilou explained that she wished to cut down, little by little, her active work in the hotel. At the same time she was extremely anxious that the personal note which she had always regarded as most important – 'as did your dear grandfather' – should not be lost.

'Your darling mother had great charm, and so did you,

as a child. I'm sure, too, from the brief letters I've had from you along the years – on birthdays and at Easter – that you have also inherited her genuinely sweet disposition and her capable ways.'

'I hope you're right!' Irene smiled doubtfully.

'I'm sure I am. Anyway, when, last year, the doctor told me I must take things more easily, I refused to listen to suggestions from David and others about competent young women who would like to work here. I thought to myself: "Irene, my grandchild, is the one I want. She will be twenty-one soon, and free to do as she pleases, for herself, and the little girl too. On her birthday I shall write and ask her to come and make her home here." That's what I did. And here you are.'

Relief swept over Irene like a flood.

'We haven't been very happy with Dad's relations,' she said frankly. 'Uncle Herbert, his brother, was kind. But his wife – this Aunt Ethel who's such an obsession with Josie! Well, before we came to live with her I don't think she'd had much contact with children; didn't realize how little she liked them.'

'That must have been dreadful! You had such loving parents.'

'It wasn't so bad for me. But Josie being so much younger, it would have had quite a serious effect on her, if I hadn't been around to – to cherish her. She clings to me too much, I know. But that's why it is.'

Mrs. Vassilou nodded slowly. Then she said: 'I wasn't, of course, at all sure you'd accept my invitation. I thought you might be considering marrying someone in England. You're a beautiful girl, just as your mother was. Even more so, perhaps, with those blue eyes which make such a lovely contrast with dark hair. Not likely to lack admirers.'

Irene might have smiled at the old-fashioned phrase which went so naturally with her grandmother's correct but rather stilted English. But her thoughts had rushed again to Guy, who had been so loving, so sweet – so eager to make her his wife – until he had been pulled up short by what he had chosen to call her 'impossible conditions'.

Her eyes filled with tears.

'There was someone,' she said. 'I expected to be writing to you to announce my engagement at Christmas. But it fell through.'

The old lady did not miss the effort she was making to keep her emotion in check.

'Poor child,' she said gently. 'One day you shall tell me all about it. But now you are tired. Go upstairs and try to sleep away your fatigue.' And she added with a smile: 'You remember how we rely on siesta out here. So – for an hour or so—'

Later that day Irene and Josie went out to explore the colourful and fragrant garden, Josie skipping about like a young kid, Irene taking a more leisurely pace. She was still tired, more from the reaction of the troublous months since her birthday than from the actual journey with its delays and frustrations.

She was thankful that her grandmother was encouraging her to wait awhile before going over to visit the newer part of the Hermes, where guests were now housed. She needed time to unwind.

She had the feeling, too, that she might encounter difficulties, starting work there, even as her grandmother's assistant. David could hardly be blamed for resenting her presence; he must have felt humiliated by the old lady's keeping him in the dark about her plan. If he were to take it out of her, even in the quietest, most unobtrusive way, there wouldn't be much happiness ahead for her and Josie.

And then she told herself she was a fool to worry. Surely she wasn't so supine as to wilt over a spot of hostility which time, no doubt, would remove.

Certainly he wasn't exactly gracious in his manner, this David. But if she proved to him that she wasn't a useless amateur, who had to be 'carried' because of her relationship to his employer, things should go smoothly enough.

Why shouldn't she, after all, be an asset to the Hermes? The shipping firm in London where she had been working had certainly considered her both pleasant in manner and competent. Guy's father, the chairman of the company, though a somewhat intimidating person in office hours, had always been generous with praise.

On the third evening, when Josie was asleep upstairs, and she and her grandmother were chatting over a glass of Commanderie – that full sweet wine first made by the Crusaders during their time in Cyprus – she nerved herself for some blunt speaking. She asked forthrightly if David knew that she would be working at the Hermes.

'He does now,' was the old lady's nonchalant reply. 'You'll be under him, in a sense, you see.' And she added, with faint mischief in her dark eyes: 'He was annoyed at my not having prepared him for it. But I know David pretty well by now. I guessed him to be making plans of his own, so decided to face him with a *fait accompli*.'

Irene looked dismayed.

'Do you mean that he had found someone else?'

'I do indeed. He wanted to promote our present secretary-receptionist, Mrs. Cipriani, to the post of assistant manageress right away. Suggested that with extra training and polish from me she could be the very one to take over from me on my retirement – which I admit can't be postponed for many years longer.'

'Perhaps he's right. I certainly interviewed quite a lot of callers for my boss in London, but hotel guests are quite a different cup of tea. Maybe she'd be far more capable – and suitable – than me.' Irene's heart was descending to her boots, as the prospect of a secure and happy home for herself and Josie started to fade. 'To bring me in, and put me in a superior position, just because I'm your relation—'

Mrs. Vassilou shook her head decisively.

'My dear, I've told him plainly, more than once, that Delphine would never make the grade – as I saw it. He's sorry for her – a widow with a young child – and so am I. And she's certainly capable – ticks over like a first-class machine. But how could she take my place, as she would naturally expect to do eventually, when she doesn't like people?'

'Couldn't David supply what's wanting in that direction? Or is a woman essential?'

A slightly sardonic smile appeared on her grandmother's face.

'David's clever as they come, and as straight as a die. But he's inherited his excellent father's dourness, and precious little of his mother's charm. Under his and Delphine's joint management the Hermes would soon lose what your dear grandfather and I always considered one of the most important qualities of a good hotel – the personal touch which show people that they are remembered and welcomed as individuals.'

Irene hesitated, then asked: 'Does Mrs. Cipriani know what David was intending?'

Mrs. Vassilou shrugged her shoulders.

'Most improbable. David's an oyster – even to people whom he likes best. But that doesn't mean she hasn't her eye on the job.' And then she added, more to herself than to Irene: 'It's odd she's so hard. Her little boy – he lives in Kyrenia with her mother – is a nice child, but she doesn't spend nearly as much time with him as she could.'

And then, reminded of another child, she switched on to the subject of Josie's education. Before sending the little girl to a local school she needed to be pampered and petted until she lost her nervous look, gained colour and put on more weight. And while this was going on she must have the chance to pick up reasonable fluency in Greek. This would be easy to arrange. One of the guests, an Englishwoman who had spent many years in Greece as a governess, and who was now too old for a regular job, was apt to find time hanging on her hands. She wasn't really poor. The wealthy family for whom she had worked in Athens, teaching two generations, had given her a pension. But she loved children, liked teaching them, and had formed a small class among 'foreigners' living in the neighbourhood. She would certainly welcome Josie and prepare her in a very few months for regular attendance at an excellent school in Kyrenia.

Here was a big problem solved, Irene felt – remembering with irony Aunt Ethel's diatribes on the selfishness she was showing by making a disastrous break in Josie's education.

With Mrs. Vassilou, to decide was to act. A telephoned invitation brought Miss Taylor across to join them in a glass of wine and, meeting her, Irene felt doubly happy about the arrangement. Miss Taylor, small and thin, and rather old-fashioned in her dress, had bright, intelligent brown eyes, full of kindness and humour. There would be few tears among her pupils, but plenty of smiles and, Irene guessed, the eagerness to learn which a really good teacher usually induced. Certainly it would be impossible to imagine her speaking of any child as a brat.

A day or two later, after siesta time, Mrs. Vassilou took Irene into the main part of the hotel on a tour of inspection. In spite of its modern look it was, as Irene had confidently expected, furnished in excellent taste, with the emphasis on space so necessary in a warm climate, and on the comforts which tourists nowadays expected. The staff had the smiling good manners and friendliness which even now she could remember as characteristic of the Cypriots, and the spotlessness which everywhere met her eyes was evidence of their pride in their work, and their high standard of training.

Everything pleased her, till finally, in her grandmother's wake, she penetrated to a little room behind the office where David and the girl called Delphine Cipriani had already foregathered for tea. And now she was struck by a sense of chill.

David's manner was ordinary enough – not particularly friendly, but certainly not hostile. But Delphine, a petite and slender brunette, around thirty, by the look of her – Irene just didn't take to her. Her smile was artificial. It went no farther than her thin, well-shaped lips, leaving her light-brown eyes – was watchful the right

29

word?

'And how can I blame her if she's suspicious of me?' Irene thought, suddenly sorry for her. 'Even if David has said nothing to her of Granny's plans for me, she's no fool. She'll have guessed what's in the wind.'

A casual onlooker might have been unaware of tension in that little room, as the four of them drank their tea and exchanged polite platitudes, now in Greek, now in English. But Irene, like her small sister keenly sensitive to atmosphere, made up her mind to tackle David on the subject.

She would never, she knew, be able to work where her presence was resented, where she was regarded as an interloper. She must find out from David just where she stood. To rely entirely on reassurances from her grandmother might land her in difficulties which she had not the temperament to deal with.

And then she gave a momentary shiver. This grandmother of hers had always, by repute, liked her own way.

'If I turn down this marvellous offer of hers,' she wondered suddenly, 'will she take offence? Shall I have to return ignominiously to England?'

Surely not, she thought. There must be other jobs in Cyprus for which she was suited by training and experience, jobs which might even make it possible for her to continue living with Josie at the Hermes, giving their grandmother warm affection if not actually working for her.

Her chance to talk to David alone came quite soon when, at Mrs. Vassilou's suggestion, he took her down to the cool, spacious cellar where wines for the restaurant were kept. The romantic names thrilled her. Such names, for instance, as some of the vintage claret bore – Aphrodite – Othello! But she had to admit reluctantly, as he spoke with pride, with tenderness, almost, of the treasures stored here in bottles and casks, that apart from the delicious Commanderie to which her grandmother had introduced her, she had little experience of Cyprus wines.

'Didn't your parents let you try any?'

'I was a schoolgirl when they died, and living in England. Soft drinks were my tipple. Since I've been older, and going around a bit' – her thoughts rushed back to Guy and his preferences – 'I've learnt to like hock as well as anything.'

'We must see if we can't enlarge your tastes,' he told her pleasantly. 'Incidentally, my parents, who live down in Limassol, are experts on our local products. It's the centre of the wine trade there, and my father's job is connected with it. Your grandmother has great faith in his judgment. She and your grandfather were buying through him long before I came to work at the Hermes.'

'I suppose Delphine has picked up a lot of information!'

'Yes, indeed. Also, unlike you and me, who are half-and-halfers, she's a full-blooded Cypriot, used to the taste of wine since childhood.' He paused, then added, in a more stilted tone: 'She's a highly intelligent young woman. Invaluable here, in my estimation.'

Irene said nothing just then, but when they came up the stone stairs and emerged into the sunshine, she remarked abruptly: 'You want her to carry on in management with you when my grandmother eventually retires. That's so, isn't it?'

He was taken aback for a second, then he shrugged his broad shoulders.

'I'm no good at feminine fencing,' he said. 'I admit that for some time I've hoped, and imagined, that things would work out that way. I've given a lot of time and trouble to training her. However, if your grandmother wishes me to start all over again with you, I shall naturally do my best. She's been very generous to me and my family.'

'Perhaps I should refuse her offer,' Irene said quietly. 'I don't care for the idea of being foisted on you, just because I'm a relation. Displacing a far more competent woman – a widow with a child, what's more.'

31

'It wouldn't help,' he told her shortly. 'According to your grandmother you have a quality which Delphine and I lack – and that's charm, combined with a genuine liking for people. Your mother had it, and so of course has she herself. Unless someone in authority has it, a hotel will founder, efficiently notwithstanding. That's her firm opinion.'

She would not stoop to flatter him – to pretend to him that he had a large measure of social gifts. She simply asked unhappily: 'If I fall in with Granny's idea, what will happen to Delphine?'

'She'll stay on, I hope. Your grandmother has nothing but praise for her as a book-keeper and stenographer – and other things on the practical side.'

And then along the path came the girl they were talking about, looking unnaturally pale.

'I've just had a telephone message that Theo's not well,' she said a little breathlessly. 'May I have the evening off, please, to go to him?'

'Of course.' David was immediately sympathetic. 'And if you want to be away longer, or bring the kid here—'

'I shan't, I'm sure. It's just my mother's fussing.' And then she turned to Irene. 'There's a great bunch of stephanotis arrived for you by special messenger,' she said curtly. 'You'll find it in the office.'

Irene was aware of David's swift, surprised glance, but the next instant his attention was all for Delphine again.

'You look rotten,' he exclaimed. 'White as a sheet. I'm going to give you a nip of brandy and run you home.' And to Irene he observed over his shoulder, as he moved off: 'I'll be back soon, but see what you can do in the dining-room meanwhile – even if it's only writing out the menus.'

She nodded, but was not very pleased to hear Delphine remark as she went off with David: 'I've told Nicos to write out the menus. I thought it wiser. And the table decorations—'

Irene drew a deep breath.

'You've a lot to learn, Delphine,' she thought indignantly. Then, remembering the flowers awaiting her, she made her way to the office.

They were a gift, as she had anticipated, from Andreas Nikolaides. The attached card announced it, with the added message scribbled on the back that he would be telephoning her shortly.

And though he meant nothing to her, this man met casually on the journey from England – nothing, at least, as an individual – the little attention was heart-warming after David's brusqueness and Delphine's open dislike.

She found a vase, put the flowers in water, and set them on the office desk, picked up the paper on which the chef had scrawled the menu for dinner, and wrote it out in elegant Greek on the cards which lay beside it.

She would show Delphine and David that in this short period of her return to Cyprus she had picked up the little she had forgotten of her mother's tongue.

CHAPTER TWO

LEFT on her own with the staff that evening – for David did not carry out his promise to return early – Irene quickly learned how much they appreciated her presence in the hotel. Several, including Hercules, the wizened old hall porter, remembered her parents with affection, and praised her for her resemblance to her beautiful mother so tragically lost in that terrible air-crash.

It was wonderful to have a member of the family coming into the business: a reassurance that what was best in the old ways would remain. Mr. David was, of course, a relation of the Vassilous – but far out on the fringes of the family. She, the granddaughter, was the right one to take the Old Lady's place in course of time.

She didn't, in her heart, believe that this would ever

happen, nor even that she would remain permanently in this lovely island. A spark of hope remained – ridiculous, but not to be extinguished – that Guy would gradually find the separation from her past bearing. That one day his arms would close round her again, that he would own his selfishness in trying to force Josie out of her life, that she would feel his lips pressing down again on hers. She knew that she was utterly wrong to encourage so dim and baseless a hope. That she should despise herself for her weakness. So she did. And yet, at the most unlikely moments, she would remember that ardent voice of his, pleading for understanding – for a return of the deep love which he felt for her.

Fortunately life at the Hermes would provide few opportunities for fruitless day-dreaming. She had an immense amount to learn of the workings of the hotel and of its occupants.

To her amusement Nicos was not content to show her precisely how the tables were set out in the great dining-room, or to hand over the flowers which the gardeners had sent up for her use. He insisted on giving her a thumb-nail sketch of the score or so of permanent – or semi-permanent – residents, with advice on their treatment.

There was the retired, peppery British Colonel, with his anxious-looking wife. So long as his wine was served at the right temperature, and he had a rice-pudding, made just so, every day, he gave little trouble, and his lady breathed freely. Not that he was unkind to her. He obviously loved her dearly.

Then, at this little table here, two aged English spinsters sat. Their occasional moans came when Chef was too lavish with the garlic. Whereas the Italian family near-by, who had a small business in Kyrenia, could never have enough of it.

Miss Taylor, who sat alone – she was his favourite. Quiet, dignified, and invariably pleasant in manner. She spoke several languages and was always ready to come to the help of foreigners who found themselves in

34

difficulties.

His dark, deep-set eyes alight with interest, he assured her that little Josie would enjoy studying with her. All children loved her.

Although his liking to chat held things up a little, Irene found Nicos easy to work with, and when David returned – delayed by running into their advertising agent – he commented with pleasure and faint surprise on the way things had gone.

'Your grandmother, whom I saw just now, thinks you have been working long enough,' he told her. 'She wants you to join her and Josie for supper right away. I'll carry on.'

'I'm not particularly tired,' she assured him. 'I don't want to slack.'

'Don't worry. Kyria Vassilou can be a slave-driver at times,' he said lightly. 'However, one thing is certain – if she summons any of us, we have to drop what we're doing and go to her.'

Irene found her grandmother and Josie happily engaged in finishing a jig-saw puzzle, and rejoiced at the change taking place in the little girl's manner. In Maida Vale Aunt Ethel would never have given up her obsessive hobby – the pursuit of glittering prizes – to spend even a few minutes on a game with a child. But there was far more to it than that. Josie was losing her tense expression. Freed from the fear of angry words and black looks, she could relax.

As the three of them sat at supper, Irene described her recent activities, stressing the helpfulness which the staff, Nicos especially, had shown her.

'They loved your mother, and they'll love you – the older ones, anyway,' Mrs. Vassilou said comfortably. 'But tell me, dear Irene, where are those flowers which, so a little bird tells me, were sent to you today? Aren't you going to let Josie and me share them?'

'Of course!' Irene did not even wonder how her grandmother, whose eyes were twinkling, knew of the gift;

little, she had already realized, escaped the old lady. She remarked frankly: 'As I daresay you guessed, they were a gift from that man we met on our flight from England, Andreas Nikolaides.'

'I thought it might be so. Well, that is a name extremely common in Cyprus. We don't run to a very wide variety, of either Christian or surnames.' Mrs. Vassilou paused to sip her wine, then continued serenely: 'I suppose he wishes to form a friendship with you. If you, too, wish it, the correct behaviour, as he will know, is to call on me first.'

'Oh, I don't want to get involved with him or anyone else,' Irene told her grandmother quickly. 'I'm much more interested in seeing whether I can make a success of working here, at the Hermes.'

'You must have some fun, too, my darling.' Mrs. Vassilou smiled across at her, thinking how like this girl was, with her bright, enthusiastic expression, to the adored daughter she had so tragically lost. 'But as my granddaughter, who is moreover planning to make her home in the island, you will need to learn something of our social customs – which differ a good deal, I understand, from English ways. A girl of good family would not be expected to go out alone even with a man she knew fairly well, certainly not with someone met casually, on a journey.'

Listening to all this, Josie, a shade bored, suggested running over to the office and fetching the flowers, so that they could decorate the supper-table: a suggestion welcomed by her elders who had more of these conventions to discuss.

Soon after their meal, served by a shy junior waiter, Josie went off to bed, and David came over for a cup of coffee and a business talk. His glance rested for a moment on the bowl of stephanotis, but opulent as it was he made no comment, but plunged straight into mundane matters, asking first how Panos, the new young waiter, had conducted himself.

'Just like any other beginner,' was Mrs. Vassilou's calm

reply. 'Or perhaps slightly better. Why do you ask?'

'Delphine says he's cheeky, that if he didn't happen to be a relation of Nicos he wouldn't be working here. I know what an enormous importance you give to good manners; but also how unlikely Nicos is to stand any nonsense even from his nearest and dearest. So, with your approval, we give him a further chance?'

'Of course.' Mrs. Vassilou's tone was decisive. 'The real trouble is that Delphine and Nicos dislike each other. I blame Delphine most – too touchy on the subject of her dignity.'

David's grey eyes glinted.

'I don't agree with you there. Nicos is a grand fellow, but he can be damned annoying.'

'So can we all, my dear David,' Mrs. Vassilou commented coolly. 'The Hermes wouldn't have half its vitality if we – the people running it – were all in supine agreement, a set of Yes-men.' She turned to Irene. 'What do you think, my dear?'

'Surely a certain amount of harmony is desirable?' Irene ventured – a remark which drew from her grandmother a chuckle and from David a shamefaced grin. It was plain that there was no ill-temper behind their sparring, that each had a strong streak of humour. With a little tact she should, she felt, be able to get on with both of them.

But Delphine – she just couldn't take to her. She doubted whether she ever would, try as she might to be friendly.

She gained fresh impressions of all sorts, that evening, listening to her grandmother and David arguing together: gained, too, considerable information about the working of a modern hotel from the management point of view. But after an hour or so she gradually became too sleepy to concentrate, and was glad to follow Josie to bed in the white bedroom she had occupied with her parents years ago.

To her surprise Josie was awake, lying open-eyed in the

moonlight.

'Come over, Irene,' the child whispered, sitting up in
bed. 'I want to talk to you.'

'My darling, you should be asleep.'

Irene went across and sat on the side of her little sister's
bed.

'So I have been, fast asleep. But I've been dreaming –
about Guy. Because of the flowers, I suppose. He was
always giving you flowers.'

'I know.' Irene managed to control her voice. 'But he's
not a part of our life any more. We're starting fresh now.
No more Aunt Ethel, no more Guy—'

'He was much nicer than Aunt Ethel,' Josie protested.
'You liked him a lot, I know.' She hesitated before
adding: 'I thought you would marry him one day, like in
the fairy stories you used to read to me when I was small.
That I'd be the bridesmaid. That we'd all live together in
a beautiful house with a lovely garden.'

Irene bent and kissed her.

'Grown-ups are odd,' she told her with an attempt at a
smile. 'He didn't love me quite enough. That's the true
explanation.'

'It's not what Aunt Ethel said, when she was talking
about it to her friends.'

'Darling, you shouldn't have been listening!'

'I couldn't help hearing what she said in the sitting-
room one afternoon when I was stuck in the kitchen
doing my homework. About throwing away a good offer
for a lot of sentimental nonsense.'

'Forget it, my pet.'

'All right, Irene. But I still hear you crying at night
sometimes, when you think I'm fast asleep. Not so much
as you did, though!'

'You see and hear far too much,' Irene began, but the
child pulled her down on to the pillow and hugged her.

'Never mind if Guy didn't love you enough,' she told
her. 'I love you so very, very much. More than any
grown-up man could ever do.'

No one was particularly surprised when Delphine rang up next morning to say that she would be unable to return for a day or two, her little boy still being unwell.

Nor was anyone particularly worried. If Delphine had to be away, this was the best time, when the hotel was not especially full. As for Theo's illness, one of the maids had seen him out in the street with his grandmother. The presumption was that Delphine herself was off colour and hadn't liked to say so – foolish of her, since everyone appreciated how hard she worked, and how deserving she was of a let-up.

Everything went smoothly enough, despite her absence. With Josie attending – and enjoying – Miss Taylor's class in an annexe of the hotel, Irene was free to make herself generally useful, picking up practical hints on a variety of matters from both David and her grandmother, and putting them into action.

But on the third day came a shock. While Irene and Josie were peacefully breakfasting with their grandmother, in her comfortable, old-fashioned sitting-room, David came hurrying over to announce that a sizeable party of Scandinavian tourists had just arrived without notice. Evidently their travel agency had let them down, claiming to have made a definite booking for them at the Hermes when nothing of the kind had been done.

Normally he would have been obliged to send them away, to try their luck at other hotels in the island. But it happened that there were some vacant rooms, and as this seemed a completely new connection, he wanted to make every effort to keep them.

'If only Delphine had been here,' he began, frowning. 'And Hercules: he's away sick!'

'My dear David, no one's indispensable. We'll all pull our weight. Come, children, finish your coffee, and we'll go right over. Josie can help me and the chambermaids, if she likes, until Miss Taylor is ready for her. And Irene can explain matters to these tourists.'

'Isn't that asking rather a lot of her? Even if her German is as good as Delphine's, she's had no experience of this sort of thing.'

'Irene knows Swedish,' Mrs. Vassilou told him triumphantly. 'That's so, child, isn't it?'

'I've a smattering,' Irene admitted. 'I understand it pretty well, if people don't talk too fast. But I'm far from fluent.'

'You'll do splendidly,' her grandmother assured her. 'Talking to them in their own language, even if you're stumped for a word occasionally, will delight them. Now, over we go.'

Josie was all excitement, clinging to her grandmother's arm, but Irene found it hard to conceal her apprehension. To be surrounded by a group of indignant English tourists would be bad enough. To try coping with angry and vociferous Swedes—

David, detaching her skilfully from Mrs. Vassilou and Josie as they went over to the main building, showed her an unexpected touch of sympathy.

'Don't try talking Swedish, whatever your grandmother says, if it worries you,' he counselled her. 'If you're really good at German – as Delphine is – you'll find everything plain sailing. Swedes all seem to know it. Indeed a great many of them are well up in English.'

But Mrs. Vassilou had a gift for getting her own way. Sweeping into the foyer, with her granddaughters in her wake, she announced to the little crowd, milling about there, in clear, precise German, that 'Fräulein Irene' would explain to them in their own language just what was being done for them. And with that she beamed on them, bowing gracefully, and swept upstairs, Josie still hanging on to her.

Irene found, to her surprise and relief, that her grandmother had been right in pressing her to try out her Swedish. As soon as these good-looking, vigorous young Swedes realized the effort she was making they ceased waving letters and papers at her and, calming down, began to listen to her.

Appealing to their common sense, she persuaded them that fixing the blame was not the most important thing.

What was vital was their welfare and comfort.

Fortunately the hotel was not full for the next ten days, when an influx was expected. If they would come into the dining-room, where extra tables were already being put up, they would be served with coffee and rolls, while everything possible was done to arrange their accommodation.

Mrs. Vassilou, busy upstairs directing the chambermaids, managed, with that sixth sense of hers, to discover that her elder granddaughter was making a striking success of her assignment. She was far too fully occupied to come down and praise her, however; nor, it later transpired, was she in the least surprised.

But David, when he came hurrying through the office on his way to the market, expressed an unflattering astonishment.

'I thought your grandmother was crazy to expect you to handle that lot,' he told her. 'I don't believe Delphine, for all her experience, would have done as well. She'd have tried to argue with them, not persuade them amiably into the dining-room for a badly-needed breakfast.'

She smiled. 'I've a great regard for creature comforts myself,' she said.

Finding a pile of letters to answer, she began to open them, and deal with those which presented no difficulty. She would have preferred to be doing something more active and more interesting, but until a message came down from her grandmother that the problem of bedrooms was finally solved, and she could go and announce this to the Swedish tourists, she had best, she felt, stay in the office.

It was when she was sorting a few letters at the bottom of an 'In' tray that she received a shock. A typed letter on headed notepaper lay there, asking for certain reservations for a party from Sweden, with the request that if requirements could not be met a telegram should be sent immediately. A letter in plain English, with the heading that of the very agency in Stockholm with whom the new arrivals had been travelling.

She read it through a second time, noticing the date on which it had been written, and the postmark. Dispatched by air five days ago, it must have arrived on the very day Delphine had asked for leave to go home. Worry over her child must have caused her to overlook it.

She was holding it in her hand, frowning, when a shadow fell across the desk, and the next moment Delphine, to her astonishment, was standing beside her.

'This is a surprise, Delphine,' she observed, unable to conceal her embarrassment. 'I hope it means that Theo is better.'

'Let's drop pretence,' was the other girl's sharp response. 'As soon as I heard of the arrival of the Swedish party in Kyrenia – which I did half an hour or so ago – I dropped everything and drove up to see what I could do to help. Also, happening to remember something, I wanted to reach my desk before you could start rummaging.'

'If you're upset at my finding this letter—' Irene began quietly. But before she could say that she had had no intention of showing it to her grandmother or to David, Delphine had swooped, and snatched it out of her hand.

'Letters go astray in the post sometimes,' she told Irene savagely, as she tore the flimsy sheet into fragments. 'And let me tell you this – if you try telling David, or even your grandmother, that I've acted this way, they won't believe you. I've never, in all my time here, made one serious mistake.'

'All the more reason for being frank with them now,' Irene suggested. 'In any case, there's little harm done. The whole party is being fitted in. You look terribly white and tired. Why don't you go home?'

'And leave you to stab me in the back – tell them of your wonderful find?'

Irene gave her a level look. 'People are apt to judge others by their own standards,' she remarked, and leaving Delphine in possession of the office, walked across to the dining-room.

A set of indignant Swedes would be pleasanter company than Delphine Cipriani with her viper's tongue.

And as it turned out the tourists, optimistic now that all would go well for them, proved very friendly indeed. It was grand to meet a lady who spoke their language so well, and who showed such concern for them. When they returned to Sweden, after what would surely be the grandest ever holiday in Cyprus, they would tell their friends that the hotel on which they must pin their faith was undoubtedly the Hermes.

Caught up in helping Nicos and his underlings behind the scenes, Irene was astonished – and relieved, too – to find when she returned to the foyer that there was no sign of Delphine. Instead her grandmother was presiding over the office, sitting queen-like at the desk, with Chef standing beside her. Both looked up and smiled as Irene approached.

'We're making last-minute alterations to suit the newcomers,' Mrs. Vassilou told her, and Chef added, black eyes flashing: 'They have good appetites, the Swedes. Why Miss Delphine interfere – tell me I too extravagant? I know my job when she still in her cradle!'

'Mrs. Cipriani isn't well. It was good of her to come in at all,' Mrs. Vassilou told him reprovingly. And to Irene she added: 'She was looking so ill, I sent her home. She didn't want to go – she has this exaggerated sense of duty. I had to insist on it.'

The telephone rang just then and Mrs. Vassilou motioned to Irene to deal with it. She stepped into the office and took up the receiver – and then was glad she had answered it herself. For it was Andreas at the other end, with a pressing invitation to her to go dancing with him the following evening.

'I'm sorry, it's out of the question,' she told him quickly. 'We're extremely busy here. I couldn't possibly be spared.'

'Then some other evening – very soon,' he pleaded. 'I

43

so long to see you.'

Embarrassingly aware that Andreas's voice over the telephone was probably audible to the others, Irene shot her grandmother a doubtful glance.

'Tell the young man that you do not behave in this free-and-easy way,' Mrs. Vassilou exclaimed in a penetrating whisper. 'If he wishes to make your acquaintance, he must act correctly and call on me one afternoon.'

Amused, Irene found that she did not have to convey this message in full.

'My grandmother prefers—' she began.

'Okay! I can guess the rest.' She could visualize his cheerful grin. 'Did you get the flowers all right?'

'I did, indeed. Thank you very much.'

'Glad you liked them. Well, give my compliments to Kyria Vassilou and say it will be an honour to make her acquaintance. My apologies, too, for unconventional behaviour. But I've been away from Cyprus so many years I've rather forgotten our fine old-world courtesies.'

And with that he rang off.

'Rather a cheeky young man, by what I caught of his conversation,' was Mrs. Vassilou's comment. 'If I know anything of the type, he'll be on my doorstep this very afternoon.'

A remark which brought the sympathetic observation from Chef, as he smiled at Irene: 'And who could blame him.'

She smiled back at him, as memories stirred of those days when she had lived in Cyprus with her parents. People who worked for one had no idea of subservience. They regarded themselves as one of the family. It came naturally to them to speak their minds.

Although Mrs. Vassilou's action in sending Delphine home meant that Irene had to come on duty again, she was so glad of the girl's absence, that the extra work meant nothing to her.

There was, indeed, a great deal for her to do which to

44

Delphine would have been simply routine. Delphine was well accustomed to the sudden arrival of large parties, these days of tourism, though not, as on this occasion, without any notice at all. She could work with lightning speed, providing Nicos with precisely what he needed in the way of extra napery – the silver was his own concern – arranging the candles and flowers well enough to pass Mrs. Vassilou's critical eye.

But Irene, slower certainly than Delphine, did well enough to win some welcome praise from David, when her long working day neared its end.

'You've done splendidly,' he told her in that abrupt way of his, as he accompanied her back to the wing which her grandmother occupied. 'Mrs. Vassilou and I are in warm agreement over that. We only differ in one respect. I'm surprised at the way you've managed. She isn't.'

'I made quite a few mistakes,' she admitted. 'Nicos had to hand me back some tablecloths and napkins that needed darning. He was very nice about it. But he must have thought me careless.'

'That was nothing. What impressed me especially was the way you kept your temper when some of the more tiresome old residents tracked you down with ridiculous complaints.'

She laughed. 'There are plenty of occasions in a London shipping office when one could get irritated. People can be most unreasonable. But these old dears – it's just that they don't want to be overlooked when a lot of strangers come along.'

'I can see you're going to pamper them, the way your grandmother does,' was his reply to this. 'Though, mind you, she can get tough if anyone, staff or visitor, really plays up.' And then he asked her with dry amusement: 'Can you show ruthlessness, too? I should find that hard to believe!'

Her thoughts flew to Guy and his bitter accusation, and to her dismay, her mood changing, the tears rushed to her eyes.

'My dear, what have I said to hurt you?' He had

45

stopped in his tracks, his hand firm on her bare arm. For the light shining from over her grandmother's front door made her distress all too evident.

'I'm a fool, that's all,' she stammered. 'Remembering something I ought to forget. And maybe I'm a little tired.'

On the edge of asking gently: 'Something – or some-one?' his Scots blood asserted itself. One did not go prying into other people's emotional concerns, even those of close friends, let alone those of a stranger. Instead, he said: 'We've overworked you badly today – ever since you've been here, in fact. It's high time you had a let-up, and a little fun.' Then, because she was still dabbing at her eyes, he added: 'What about a few minutes in the fresh air before you go in?'

She knew what he was leaving unsaid: 'You don't want your grandmother and little sister to see you've been crying.' And she was grateful to him.

Clearly he wasn't as crude as she had thought. Indeed with all his brusqueness, his bouts of impatience, this big, hulking man was capable of a wholly unexpected delicacy. Strolling with her round the moonlit garden, fragrant with citrus blossom and with other flowers which she could not identify, he apologized awkwardly for his un-welcoming attitude to her on her arrival.

'I love your grandmother dearly, respect her for her practical good sense. But when she rides roughshod over me, as she sometimes does, I get mad, especially when I think she's making a serious mistake.'

'I can understand that. You probably thought that, ig-norant as I was – and am – of the hotel business, I'd be a damned nuisance.'

'I'm afraid I did. You see, out here in the Middle East, there's an almost suffocating sense of family. Inex-perienced people are brought into a business simply be-cause they happen to be relations in need of a job.' And then he laughed, a shade self-consciously: 'Which, to tell you the truth, is just what happened to me, when I had that accident and had to quit the Merchant Navy. I had

46

hardly left hospital in Southampton and come out to convalesce with my parents in Limassol when the Vassilous were in contact with us, inviting us all three for a holiday at the Hermes, and then offering me a job. Fortunately your grandfather lived long enough to give me some valuable training.'

'And fortunately for my grandmother you accepted their offer.' Irene spoke with warm sincerity. And she asked hesitantly: 'Do you miss the sea much, David?'

'Oh, I've got a boat, of sorts. I go sailing sometimes. I'll take you and Josie out one day, if you're not nervous.' He gave a slight chuckle. 'I've invited Delphine once or twice, but she's far too scared.'

The mention of Delphine was like a chill little breeze.

'She's the one I'm sorry for,' Irene said. 'It's hard on her, my coming here out of the blue.'

'Looking at it in a detached way, if it had to happen, better now than later, from her point of view,' was David's blunt comment. 'If she doesn't want to stay on, now that the highest promotion seems unlikely, she can easily get another good post in the island.'

'Or she might marry,' Irene ventured. 'She's a very pretty woman.'

He shrugged his heavy shoulders. 'There seems to be some mystery about her husband's death, over in Greece, and maybe because of that she seems very averse to leading a normal social life.'

'Perhaps the job here, and the possession of an adored child, are enough interest for her.'

'I daresay. Anyway, she's hardly encouraging to admirers!'

It occurred to Irene to wonder if David himself was in that category. He hardly acted like a man in love. Yet with his inherited prudence he might have been looking forward to running the Hermes eventually, with Delphine as his wife and helpmate. He evidently thought highly of her capabilities – was clearly fond of her, in his matter-of-fact, unromantic way.

And then another thought came to her – so ridiculous that she nearly laughed out loud. Suppose her grandmother, spinning plans in that active brain of hers, should try some match-making between herself and David, so that the Hotel Hermes should belong for the foreseeable future to actual members of 'the Family'.

'What are you giggling about now, you creature of moods?' David demanded good-humouredly.

'Something utterly preposterous,' she told him flippantly. But already sadness was returning, justifying his accusation.

To think of marriage, even in such a ridiculous context, brought the sharp reminder that only a few months ago she had been dreaming of her wedding day, of a rosy future with a man whose smile, whose voice, whose lightest touch had power to stir her heart. Someone who made every other man she met seem utterly without attraction – for her, at least.

He told her next day, when they were going through the morning mail together, that with her grandmother's approval he would be contacting Delphine, and suggesting her returning to work on the following Monday, bringing her little boy with her.

'He's a nice kid, and it's good for him to come up here and have the freedom of the grounds. His grandmother's kind, but too fussy, worries Delphine unnecessarily. She'll be better if she has him under her own eye for a spell.'

'It's a fine idea,' was Irene's quick response, and she spoke in all sincerity. For surely Delphine, with her child around, would show a more human side. He might get in her way in working hours, but perhaps Josie could help here, take him over sometimes and play with him. At school, in London, teachers had declared that she was 'sweet' with smaller children. Though Aunt Ethel had seen to it that she had no chance of exercising her gifts in this direction – 'brats' of all ages being firmly discouraged from showing their noses at the house in Maida Vale.

There was still, in Delphine's absence, more than enough work for her. Tourists spent the daylight hours, very often, in visiting beauty spots or places of historical interest, in distant parts of the island. But the young Swedes were more interested in staying nearer home, swimming and surfing and sunbathing. They were usually in at lunch-time as well as for all other meals and, with casual visitors dropping in at midday, to sample Chef's noted delicacies, the restaurant was full to overflowing, which was excellent for trade but, in Irene's secret opinion, pretty exhausting.

Sunday, however, brought a slight respite. The Swedes, feeling it was time they imbibed a little culture, cleared off by hired coach to visit Famagusta, on the east coast, scene of bloody conflict between Moslem and Christian, centuries ago, and Salamis, famous for the presence of St. Paul, and his ill-treatment there, in even earlier times.

The day brought, too, a minor excitement. Andreas arrived in a fine car to call on Mrs. Vassilou – handsome, well set up, with the excellent manners characteristic of Cypriots in general.

Josie, seeing him first, rushed to greet him, calling to Irene to follow her. But Irene had learned by now something of the conventions to be observed, and remained demurely in the sitting-room with her grandmother until Josie brought him in.

Mrs. Vassilou's reception of him was formal, but Irene had expected that. The old lady would want to know a good deal about himself and his family before giving her approval to any sort of friendship between him and her granddaughter.

Although his people had lived in Nicosia at one time she knew them only as occasional visitors at the Hermes – and that some years ago. As for himself, she was politely interested in learning why he had, in recent years, spent so much time abroad.

In England her curiosity would have been regarded as discourteous, and Irene herself felt embarrassed by it. Not so Andreas. He had evidently come prepared for a cat-echism of this kind and his replies came without the least sign of resentment, or indeed, hesitation.

He left after the correct half-hour call, with Mrs. Vassilou's gracious confirmation that he would be taking her two granddaughters out for a drive on the following Tuesday afternoon. The old lady even, by a slight movement of her head, conveyed to Irene permission to join Josie in seeing him to his car.

He gave Irene a whimsical look, as he said good-bye, holding her hand a fraction longer than necessary.

'Will you ever get used to Cyprus conventions?' he asked. 'I find it difficult to swallow them myself, after years abroad, and I'm a Cypriot, born and bred. Still, it can be fun evading them. Until Tuesday – Beautiful!'

And with that he was off.

'Granny, he called Irene beautiful, but isn't he handsome himself? Josie demanded, darting back into the sitting-room as the big car disappeared in the distance.

'Very handsome,' Mrs. Vassilou returned coolly. 'But a little glib, I thought.'

'What's glib, Granny?'

'Quick with his answers, dear.'

'That's what Miss Taylor would like!'

'I daresay!' And then the old lady turned to Irene, who had just come in, and asked her with a slightly satiric glint in her dark eyes: 'Well, my dear, was he satisfied with taking the two of you out for a run?'

'He didn't say,' was Irene's demure reply. Her eyes, too, were smiling. 'I hardly think so. But so far as I'm concerned, it's fine.'

On Monday morning Delphine returned, bringing Theo, her small son, with her. He was a dark, good-looking boy, shy, quiet and dressed almost too neatly. It was hard, Irene thought, on her first encounter with him in the foyer, to imagine his making a nuisance of himself. He did not even cling to his mother particularly: seemed the kind of child who would be content to play by himself in a corner.

She wondered whether Delphine would show any sign of embarrassment over her behaviour the last time they had met in the office, whether the memory of snatching and destroying that letter from the Swedish Agency would give her an air of guilt. But though Delphine looked pale and tired still, her manner was blandly detached. She was, Irene thought, a consummate actress – unless she really thought that to suppress an urgent letter addressed to the hotel was unimportant.

Although there was plenty of work to be done in the office on a Monday morning, Irene did not offer to help the other girl. She had no wish to court a polite snub. Instead she followed what she had learned was her grandmother's custom – going round the public rooms with a smile for staff and visitor alike and seeing that all was going smoothly.

Presently, however, she found that she was being followed – and by Theo. She turned and held out a hand to him.

'Hello, my dear!'

He came closer, and after a moment's hesitation slipped his small hand in hers.

'Mama said to go and play quietly in her bedroom,' he told her, 'but there isn't room. They're putting up a bed for me in the corner.'

'And you want to come round with me?'

'Well, I mustn't get in the way.'

She found something touching in his old-fashioned manner. 'I don't think you'll do that,' she told him good-humouredly. 'Maybe you can help me a little, putting fresh writing-paper and envelopes on the desks – tidying up the racks with the picture postcards.'

He nodded earnestly. 'I could do that.'

'And you can smile back at everyone who smiles at you.'

He gave a grin. 'And *not* make a face at the people who look cross!'

She pinched his ear lightly. 'They need an even bigger smile,' she said.

But there were no frowns from anyone as she and Theo went around together. The Cypriot staff, loving young

51

children, were quick to make a fuss of him, and the English spinsters put down their knitting, and exclaimed that he would be a companion for Josie.

'Who's Josie?' he demanded, as they went on in search of Nicos.

'My little sister. She's older than you, so maybe you wouldn't have too much fun, playing together.'

He shrugged his shoulders. 'I don't have many boys or girls to play with,' he said nonchalantly. 'But I don't mind. I make up pretend games in my head.'

'So does Josie, I think. She's always been alone a lot.'

Before they found Nicos they ran into the old Colonel who had been described to her as 'peppery' and who was clearly struggling to keep his temper. He controlled himself enough to pat Theo amiably on the head, and then to give Irene a hardly convincing smile, before uttering his protest.

'I've been having very humiliating treatment of recent months,' he told her. 'Your grandmother made special terms for my wife and myself, in view of our living here as permanent residents. Yet as often as not my fortnightly bill is made out at the original price. Mrs. Cipriani always gives me a perfunctory apology for her mistake, and puts things right, but I'm getting a little tired of it.'

'It wouldn't be for me to say anything to her,' was Irene's quiet reply. 'I'm only a newcomer. If it keeps on happening, you might mention it either to Mr. MacLeod or to my grandmother.'

'Well, I don't want to get her into trouble.'

'You wouldn't. There's probably some simple explanation. She works very hard, and when she's busy may refer to an out-of-date ledger.'

Colonel Bykers grunted. 'I'd rather you nudged her memory yourself,' he said.

'Is he cross with my mummy?' Theo asked, as they wandered on.

'Not really. But he's been a soldier, and they like to have things just so.'

And she thought no more of the conversation.

They went out into the garden now, to collect the flowers which Hector, the whiskered old gardener, had cut for the dining-room, and ran straight into David, back from market and on his way to the kitchen.

'You're the very person I want to see,' he told Irene, in a more friendly, relaxed tone than he commonly used to her. Then, turning to Theo, he stooped down and shook hands solemnly with him.

'You're very welcome,' he told him, 'and I can see you're not wasting your time.'

'I haven't done much, Uncle David,' was the child's modest reply.

'You've persuaded a very pretty lady to let you spend most of the morning with her, haven't you?'

Irene looked at David in surprise, colouring slightly.

'Compliments! I didn't think they were at all in your line.'

'Don't forget I've Cypriot blood in my veins,' was his light response. 'Dour Scot that I may be on my father's side! But listen – now that Delphine is back, you ought to have at least an afternoon off. What about letting me take you and Josie – and this fellow, too, if he'd like to come – for a drive tomorrow afternoon? I've planned something very special.'

'Oh, David!' Her face fell. 'We've got Granny's approval for going out with Andreas Nikolaides tomorrow. He called on her yesterday, and it's all fixed up.'

'Okay. Have a good time.' His tone was cheerfully matter-of-fact, as he swung off, and plainly he was not in the least disappointed. He had just been showing conventional politeness to his employer's granddaughters, with as little real feeling as lay behind that silly compliment. Probably he was relieved to be shot of a tiresome chore.

But why, for goodness' sake, should she mind whether he was disappointed or not? Sheer feminine vanity, she supposed! After all, it was not as though she cared either

53

way herself. Not in the very least.

And then, just as she and Theo were returning to the staff quarters of the hotel, to the pantry where the flowers were to be arranged, they ran slap into Delphine, looking very annoyed indeed.

'Theo, what are you doing, making a nuisance of yourself to Miss Meredith? I told you to go and play in my bedroom.'

'They were doing things there, Mama.' His small face was downcast. 'Putting up my bed.'

'You could have gone on to the balcony,' she returned sharply, and to Irene she observed curtly: 'If he gets in the way, he won't be allowed to stay here. I have to be strict with him.'

Irene looked the other girl full in the eyes.

'He's been great company for me,' she said sincerely.

'Very kind of you,' was the cool reply. 'But he must learn to do as he's told.' And she took the boy's hand and led him off in silence.

'Not much hope of his being allowed to make friends with Josie,' Irene thought as she continued on her way to the pantry. 'Delphine's far too jealous.' It was understandable in a way, she supposed, that a young widow with an only child should feel this fierce possessiveness. But it would be difficult to explain to Josie that she must leave the little boy alone.

She sighed, as she filled a crystal vase with gloriously coloured, sweet-smelling freesias.

She had thought, back in England, that life would be simple, at least, out here, living with her grandmother. But it certainly had its complications.

CHAPTER THREE

HOWEVER, both she and Delphine had reckoned without Mrs. Vassilou.

The old lady decreed benevolently that both children

were to come to tea with her that afternoon, in order to get to know each other. After tea they could play together in the grounds. There was a wooden hut in the far corner with some old toys and games in it. Hector, the old gardener, would unlock it for them. They would find plenty to amuse them there, but they had better put on old clothes. Everything would be dusty.

Irene was delighted. Rummaging about in an old shed was just what most children would adore. But Delphine barely concealed her annoyance. Theo hadn't brought anything but his best and tidiest clothes, she murmured crossly to Irene, the next time she ran into her, adding that Mrs. Vassilou was getting more unpractical than ever in her old age, that for the sake of the hotel it was as well she had such a first-rate manager, with his head screwed on tight.

'Why not explain things to my grandmother?' Irene suggested mildly.

'And risk a snub? She's told me already that I'm obsessed with the idea of making a little gentleman of Theo – that my mother and I shouldn't try so hard to keep him out of the rough-and-tumble of life.'

'Well, leave it. We can always put his clothes into the tub if he gets in a mess.' Irene's tone was kindly. It couldn't be easy for those two women to give a small lad the ideal upbringing. He needed other boys to play with, of course. But meanwhile he and Josie – if they got on together – should enjoy their afternoon.

And they did.

Even before they had finished the fruit juice and syrupy *kateyfi* which Mrs. Vassilou had provided for them, they were putting out feelers of friendship. Josie's Greek was far better than Theo's scrappy English, but with both of them constantly making mistakes there was much laughter.

'They'll learn from each other more quickly than in any school,' Mrs. Vassilou murmured to Irene, who had dropped in for tea. 'We must see that they have plenty of opportunity for playing together. Delphine is absurdly

55

possessive, poor girl, but if she finds that the boy is picking up English quickly from Josie, she'll look at things differently.'

Exploring that disused shed in the grounds gave the two children enormous pleasure. All the best garden furniture had been removed the previous year to a new and vastly superior wooden hut, in a part of the grounds more accessible to visitors. Clubs for clock golf, tennis racquets and croquet mallets were kept there, in neat racks. But this dusty old place was a regular Aladdin's cave. Not only had shabby garden chairs and tables been stowed there, but, as Mrs. Vassilou had told them, derelict toys. A rocking-horse was the great find. Its appearance was sadly battered, the once-flowing mane reduced to a few straggling white hairs. But it still rocked satisfactorily.

Sleds, too, brought cries of excitement.

'They'd do fine if we ever went to Troodos in the winter,' Theo babbled excitedly in Greek. 'Mama says we could never afford it, but Uncle David might take us. Even with his bad foot he's good in the snow, people say.'

Josie's eyes shone. 'Maybe I could come, too. Some of the bigger girls at school went tobogganing at Hampstead one year. I was too small then.'

'Of course you could come.' He beamed at her, then quickly turned to pull out an old-fashioned oil lamp. 'We could take this up with us for picnics in the snow – heating up soup and coffee.'

'Wouldn't it blow out in the wind? Thermos jugs would be better,' Josie suggested.

The small boy shrugged his shoulders. 'Perhaps. But they'd be rather dull.'

They dragged out next an old lilo, and even when they had shaken off most of the cobwebs it didn't look up to much.

'We *could* get Panos to blow it up,' Theo mused. 'But I don't expect it's any good.'

'If it was just rubbish it would have been thrown away,' Josie maintained. 'Shall I ask Irene to try?'

56

Theo's small, pale face clouded.

'I've been thinking that your granny might let us have this hut as our secret place. If we get the grown-ups coming in—!'

'Irene isn't at all the ordinary sort of grown-up,' Josie told him loyally. 'Still, I see what you mean. Now look at this.' And she pulled out a small picnic basket, the wicker broken, and one of the straps missing. Although the outside was dirty, the contents – plastic cups and plates and cutlery – had been wrapped in paper napkins and were clean.

'We could have a feast here,' Theo exclaimed.

'Of course. But my goodness, we're going to have a lot of cleaning to do here, if the grown-ups are to be kept out.'

'Girls are always so fussy about a bit of dirt,' was Theo's aggrieved comment. 'I can't see it would take us long. There's a broom over there in that corner.'

When a church clock in the distance struck six o'clock, they returned cheerfully to Mrs. Vassilou's quarters – ready, after all that dust and exertion, for a sweet and juicy orange apiece. And at once the problem of cleaning their precious shed was taken out of their grimy hands.

'I didn't realize the hut was as bad as that.' Mrs. Vassilou, far from being angry with them for their disreputable appearance, was actually apologetic. 'I'll see that it is given a good clean-up tomorrow.'

'But, Granny, you won't have anything taken out!' Josie pleaded. 'Some of the things that look like rubbish are treasures.' She had slipped into halting Greek, and Theo broke in with a triumphant: 'I rode on the rocking-horse.'

'I'll superintend the spring-cleaning myself,' Mrs. Vassilou promised. 'And now you both need a good wash and some fresh clothes. Off with you, Theo.'

For a second he looked at Josie appealingly, as if asking her to escort him. Then, recollecting that though much younger than her, he was a boy, and she only a girl, he turned abruptly, and ran off.

'I hope his mother won't be angry with him,' Josie ventured, with memories of Aunt Ethel stirring in her brain.

Mrs. Vassilou smiled at her reassuringly, and went to the house telephone.

'I'll tell her that I'm the one she must blame,' she said. 'And now, my darling, go quickly and have a bath before Irene comes over and gets a shock.'

'*She* wouldn't scold me, Granny.' Josie's voice was confident. 'She never does. Aunt Ethel used to say she spoiled me ab-abominably.'

'Time you forgot Aunt Ethel, my dear!'

Josie, halfway through the parlour door, paused for a moment.

'I do, mostly. But she still comes into my dreams.'

Her voice was sombre, but only while she spoke. Next moment, as she disappeared up the stairs, she was singing a gay little Greek song she had picked up in Miss Taylor's class.

The following morning Mrs. Vassilou decided in her usual sudden way that she would like David to take her down to Limassol, on a wine-purchasing expedition. It was a long and tiring drive, but she had had to miss visiting his mother on her feast day, the previous month. It was high time she took her apology, and gift of chocolates, in person.

'Amaranth MacLeod is a relative of your dear grandfather's family, as you know,' she explained to Irene, adding: 'I would have taken you and Josie, but this would mean leaving Delphine on her own the whole day, and it wouldn't be fair.'

'Are you sure it won't matter going out for a drive with Andreas Nikolaides?' Irene demanded. 'I could easily postpone it.'

'If you keep it to a couple of hours, from four to six, there'll be no inconvenience to anyone,' her grandmother assured her. 'But mind, no leaving Josie behind to play with Theo. She may not be much of a chaperone, but she's better than nobody. Our Cyprus men have warmer blood than Englishmen, don't forget!'

Josie made no bones about going for this drive with 'our friend, Mr. Nikolaides,' as she called him importantly.

But Theo was sharply disappointed at the thought of being left to his own resources. Even if they had to keep away from the hut until it was cleaned there were other things he and Josie could have done together. In fact one of the chambermaids had offered to take the two of them on to the beach for the afternoon.

He hadn't cried. Young as he was, his masculine pride forbade it. But Josie, returning from 'school', saw the trembling of his lower lip, and she rushed to Irene to plead that he should be allowed to come for the drive with them.

Irene, who was sorting table linen at the time, was dubious. 'I'll ask his mother,' she promised, 'but don't raise his hopes in the meantime. She may have other plans for him.'

She finished her task, handed over the pile of snowy tablecloths and napkins to Nicos, and went to the office where Delphine was busy at the typewriter. Maybe, she thought, Delphine would welcome the idea: she was always nervous – unnecessarily so – of Theo's 'getting under the visitors' feet'. To know he was out and enjoying himself, *and* well looked after, might appeal to her.

But Delphine came out with a firm and frosty negative.

'In Cyprus we consider it the height of ill manners to fish for an invitation, either for oneself or one's children,' she declared, then added: 'I'm afraid your ideas of looking after a child don't, anyway, coincide with mine. Theo came back here yesterday, after playing with your young sister, looking like a herdsman's child who'd been out in the fields all day. I've never known him in such a filthy state.'

'Josie was in an awful mess, too,' Irene conceded

59

mildly. 'But really it was my grandmother's fault, as she's the first to admit. She sent them out, not realizing the amount of dirt and dust there.'

'Well, there'll be no question of Theo turning himself into a peasant this afternoon.' Delphine's brown eyes were as hard as pebbles. 'Even if this – this picked-up boy-friend of yours invited him, I shouldn't permit him to go. And now, please, if you don't mind, I'm extremely busy.'

And then as Irene, controlling herself with difficulty, turned abruptly away, Delphine threw one more barb.

'If you come across Theo fooling around, will you please tell him I want him at once. He's too young to be running wild. I prefer to keep him under my own eye.'

Irene came very near to saying angrily: 'If you want him, go and find him.' Delphine's attitude could hardly have been more offensive. But she bit back the words. For everyone's sake – the boy's most of all – an out-and-out row must be avoided.

He and Josie were playing together, she knew, near the old shed, where the spring-cleaning operations which Mrs. Vassilou had ordered were just being concluded. They wanted to make sure that nothing they treasured should be thrown away as rubbish. So she went straight there and telling Theo pleasantly that his mother needed him, she sent him scampering over to the office.

'Does that mean she's going to let him come with us this afternoon?' Josie demanded anxiously.

Irene shook her head. 'She wants him with her.'

'Well, I think it's a rotten shame! He's only a little boy. It's mean to disappoint him.'

Irene slipped her arm round her. 'Darling, don't take things to heart so much. One of the maids will probably be allowed to take him down to the beach. He'll enjoy that, you know.'

But Josie was not to be placated. She had lost her old submissiveness.

'I think Mrs. Cipriani is a horrid person,' she said.

There was no one around when Andreas drove up by

the side road to Mrs. Vassilou's door to collect Irene and Josie. He was in good spirits, which remained undimmed even when Irene explained that, by her grandmother's decree, they must be back in a couple of hours.

'It's much quicker getting out into the high road if you go the other way, past the main entrance,' Irene told him, as she settled in beside him, Josie climbing into the back.

For a second his glance wavered – or did she only imagine it? Probably it was only her fancy, for he returned easily enough: 'Oh, I prefer the side entrance. I still remember it as the main way in and out, before all the alterations and additions were done. I'm a bit of a sentimentalist, I suppose.'

'I, too. But with all these tourists coming, the Hermes would have been left behind if it hadn't been considerably enlarged and modernized.'

'Which would have been a great pity. If that had happened it's conceivable that you might not have come to Cyprus.'

'Oh, we'd have come out all right,' Josie piped up from the back. 'Whatever the Hermes was like – or even if Granny was living somewhere else, in a tiny little house. We'd never have stayed in Maida Vale, would we, Irene?'

Irene turned to eye her with mock severity. 'Stop thinking about Aunt Ethel,' she said.

Andreas started up now and they moved off.

'Two hours doesn't give us much time,' he observed. 'We'll have to content ourselves with a look at Nicosia. I don't suppose you've seen much of it yet.'

They hadn't. And as it turned out they did not see much of it that afternoon. Nor did they even stop long in Kyrenia, for, as Andreas pointed out, by the time they had seen half of its beauties, they would have to think about returning to the Hermes. Instead they dawdled along the mountainous road between the two towns, and now Josie was able to fulfil her ambition – get out of the car and wander about picking flowers, as she had longed

61

to do when driving with David from the airport on the morning of their arrival.

Andreas, eager to have Irene to himself for a while, was only too glad to deposit the little girl on the hillside, and for a short time she stayed with him in the car chatting about nothing in particular. Not for a moment did she let Josie out of her sight, and when Andreas' arm stole round her, and his voice took on an amorous tone, she decided it was time to join her. His immediate reaction was to tighten his hold on her, but when he saw that he was beginning to annoy her, he reluctantly let her go, and reaching across opened the door for her.

'We'll all pick flowers,' he said lightly. 'And perhaps one day, if I'm patient, I may pluck the loveliest one I've ever seen – a white rose!'

She chose to ignore what she considered his sentimental nonsense, deciding that if he persisted in it she would have to put an end to their friendship. It was a pity. He was a likeable young man in some ways, and it was pleasant to have one acquaintance, at least, outside the Hermes circle. But she was not going to get involved in anything that even looked like a romance. Some women, perhaps, could tumble out of one love affair into another. She was not one of them. Weak it might be, but Guy still held a place in her foolish heart. She wanted no one else's kisses.

But Andreas, amorous though he might be, had tact.

Climbing with her and Josie on that short, blossom-studded turf, he had much of interest to tell them. From where they stood they could see, perched high on a craggy peak, the castle of St. Hilarion, and he became genuinely eloquent as he explained its history – how this and the other castles perched perilously on the heights of the Kyrenia range had originally been built as watch-towers by the Byzantines against their Saracen foes. How long ago? Well, they had certainly been there when Richard Coeur de Lion invaded the island and married the beautiful Princess Berengaria.

In later times they had for a few centuries been used as

castles to live in, and a few years ago, one of them – Buffavento, the Deifier of Winds – had figured in the famous film of *Snow White and the Seven Dwarfs*.

Listening to all this, Josie forgot to look for fresh flowers. 'When can we have a whole day to go exploring?' she demanded.

'Before long, if Irene agrees – and if we can both get the time off from work,' was Andreas' answer. But a moment later, Josie having wandered out of earshot, to get a better view of what was truly a magnificent scene, he asked urgently: 'And when can we go out together, you and I, without our young chaperone?'

'When the moon turns blue,' was her light answer. 'Here, in my Cypriot grandmother's home, I follow the conventions with which my mother was brought up.'

'But you're over twenty-one!'

She laughed, determined to keep the conversation on a flippant level.

'You know how much that counts, out here. Of course, when I get to thirty—'

He pretended to scowl. 'Cypriot men are not like your cool Britons,' he said – using almost the same words as her grandmother. 'It's dangerous to tease them!'

But Irene suddenly had something else to think about. It had occurred to her to glance at her watch, and she saw to her dismay that it was nearly six o'clock – the hour when she should be back at the Hermes, helping Delphine – and Nicos, too, most likely.

'We must go,' she said hurriedly. 'I should be on duty at the hotel by now.' And she called to Josie to come quickly.

But Josie, though still not far away, had climbed up some rocks and found it a slower and more perilous business getting down again. Indeed one of those distant, invisible church clocks had sent its six silvery notes into the quiet air before the child was tucked once more into the back of the car.

'We shan't be all that late,' Andreas promised. 'If we were, it's hardly likely the proprietor's granddaughter would get into trouble.'

'The time just rushed by,' Josie declared. '*Didn't* it, Irene?'

'Yes, it did,' Irene returned frankly, and was hardly surprised when Andreas greeted this remark by taking her hand in his for a moment, and pressing it hard. Even 'a cool Briton' would surely have done as much.

Arriving late meant, inevitably, a dose of unpleasantness from Delphine. She greeted Irene, who came running over to help her, with the cold observation that she herself had coped with the work, made more difficult by the fact that Nicos and Chef had had a quarrel.

'There's absolutely nothing for you to do,' she ended.

'But there still would have been time for me to get around,' Irene protested. 'You needn't have rushed like this.'

'Someone has to have a sense of responsibility,' was Delphine's stiff rejoinder. 'I couldn't take any risk. When a girl of your age goes out with a new and exciting boyfriend, it's only natural she should forget the time.'

Irene choked back her anger. After all, she had put herself in the wrong by her carelessness.

'I'm sorry to have given you trouble.' Try as she might to sound calm and dignified, her voice was as chilly as Delphine's. Then she asked shortly: 'What were Nicos and Chef fighting about?'

Delphine shrugged her shoulders.

'I neither know nor care,' she said. 'And I strongly advise you to keep out of it, too.'

When Irene went across to the dining-room, determined, in spite of Delphine's discouragement, to see if there was still anything she could do to help Nicos, she found that there was only one thing he wanted – sympathy!

It seemed that Mrs. Vassilou had given orders, before she left for the Limassol trip, that a tray of cold food – chicken and ham, and a very special salad for which Chef was famous – should be taken over to her own dining-room, so that she and David could have a quiet meal together when they came in. Unfortunately Nicos had been late in passing the precise order on to Chef who, by the time he received it found himself lacking one of the most important ingredients for his salad.

Without it, he declared, the meal would have no distinction. But fortunately the situation could be saved. He was serving for the guests' dinner a casserole of such novelty and excellence that he could not endure the thought of Kyria Vassilou missing the enjoyment of it. Nor did he intend that she should.

'Cold chicken and ham!' He had almost spat the words out in his contempt, Nicos told Irene in shocked tones.

'I tell him he is a fool,' Nicos continued. 'Who is to stay up and bring his precious casserole across to Kyria Vassilou late tonight – as it well might be? He himself cannot. Nor can I. He is my brother-in-law and we have to attend a family council tonight over a division of family property. Who else can we trust? No one! We should do as Kyria Vassilou says and take the tray of chicken and ham over to her dining-room right away.'

'Chicken and ham *and my special salad*!' came a roar from the doorway, and there stood Chef exploding with fury. 'Miss Irene, this stupid fellow tells me too late what the Kyria orders. And when I wish to substitute a most beautiful and novel dish, he makes a thousand difficulties.'

'It's easy to keep a casserole hot,' Irene observed mildly.

'But who is to be trusted to wait up for her?' Nicos demanded. 'Any of the staff who are our relatives must come to this family council. Who does that leave? A few juniors from the kitchen – to gobble up half of it, as like as not, or drop it on the way over, if they don't clear off and go to bed before the Kyria comes.'

Before Chef could argue the matter farther, Irene took command.

'You'll have to trust me,' she told them firmly. 'Send the casserole over directly after dinner, and I'll keep it hot in my grandmother's own oven. But the tray of chicken and ham must come over as well. Elderly ladies cannot always take rich food late at night.'

To her immense relief – for she had visualized the discussion going on interminably – the two men accepted her solution with philosophic shrugs, their truce being helped by the fact that it was now close on the dinner hour, and high time they were at their respective posts.

At least, she felt, she had done something to atone for coming in late!

It was nearly eleven when her grandmother and David returned, and it was clear at once that they appreciated her serene and smiling welcome, and the trouble she had taken over their meal. Sensibly she said nothing of the disagreement between Chef and Nicos. Nor, as she had anticipated, did her grandmother comment on the arrival at table of the casserole. The old lady settled for a minute helping of cold food, while David, having failed to persuade Irene even to take a glass of wine or a biscuit, ate heartily of Chef's masterpiece. And all the while, Mrs. Vassilou talked of the splendid trip they had had – of the eagerness David's parents had shown to make the acquaintance of herself and Josie.

'My mother knew yours very well.' David managed to get a word in. 'I hadn't realized just how friendly they were, as girls. I must certainly take you and Josie over there one of these days, if you can spare time from your various commitments.'

'Don't be absurd, David. Of course Irene can spare the time.' Kyria Vassilou's tone was impatient. 'She has not come here to be a drudge. She is to enjoy herself, have a happy life, as well as to train in hotel management.'

'Of course!' David sipped his wine thoughtfully; then held his glass to the light. 'This last consignment of Othello is remarkably good, makes a fine accompaniment to Chef's excellent casserole.' Adding after a moment, looking straight at Irene: 'Any girl with her attractions isn't likely to miss out in fun. She'll be very much in demand.'

66

Mrs. Vassilou chuckled at that. 'You see, Irene, he's not wholly Scottish. He can pay a woman a compliment without choking over it.'

'I was stating a fact, not buttering her up,' David returned easily, and sipped his wine again.

Irene, who had coloured under his steady look, addressed herself to her grandmother. 'I'm having a very happy life here,' she said.

Mrs. Vassilou nodded complacently, but David asked, almost too cordially: 'Did you have a pleasant time with Nikolaides?'

'Yes, indeed!' Irene had regained complete command of herself now. After all, she wasn't a schoolgirl to be discomposed because of the way a man looked at her. And she told them both lightly how she and Josie had picked anemones and cyclamen on the slopes of the Kyrenia foothills, and listened to Andreas' stories of the old castles perched as though by witchcraft on their seemingly inaccessible crags.

'The time rushed by, and I'm afraid we were a little late getting back,' she ended. 'All the same I'd have had time to get through all my usual jobs if Delphine hadn't been so conscientious and done them herself.'

'You don't mention Theo having gone with you,' Mrs. Vassilou observed suddenly. 'I hope Delphine gave him permission?'

Irene shook her head.

'Andreas would have been very willing to have him, I'm sure. But Delphine wouldn't let me ask him – told me that I didn't understand Cypriot conventions. No, manners was actually the word she used.'

'As you've just implied, Delphine is over-conscientious,' David said uncomfortably. 'And she seems a bundle of nerves, these days.'

'She ought to remarry,' Mrs. Vassilou declared. 'Then she wouldn't be so prickly – and so possessive over Theo. Some kind, steady fellow. I'd provide the dowry, if she brought a suitable man along.'

'Someone you thoroughly approved of, you mean,

Kyria!' David spoke dryly.

'Of course. And I must confess I haven't seen the right one yet.'

She spoke with an emphasis that startled Irene, but if David noticed this he gave no sign. With that bland look he could sometimes assume, he said calmly: 'Or maybe haven't recognized him as such.' Then, turning to Irene, he went on: 'Won't you at least have a little fruit? Or even half a glass of this delicious Othello? The perfect end to a perfect day!'

But Mrs. Vassilou shook her sculptured silvery head.

'What Irene needs is to catch up with her beauty sleep,' she decreed. 'Off with you, my dear. We'll clear up.' And when Irene rose obediently – being, indeed, very tired by now – and kissed her, she added warmly: 'I'm pleased with you, my dear. You're just the girl I hoped you'd be.'

She looked across to David as though for confirmation. But David, who had got to his feet and moved towards the door, was smiling whimsically.

'You've never said anything so nice to me in all the years I've been with you,' he commented. Then, as he opened the door for Irene, he lifted her hand and dropped a kiss on it. 'Just Cypriot manners,' he said.

She found Josie fast asleep; heart-breakingly sweet she looked in the moonlight, her dark lashes curled against her cheeks, a faint suggestion of a smile on her lips.

Suddenly Irene's thoughts flew back to that night on the plane, to the concern she had felt for her cherished little sister. Josie had slept restlessly in that waiting-room chair, but it hadn't only been discomfort which had given her that troubled expression.

'All my efforts hadn't saved her from nervous fears, from the misery of knowing herself disliked,' she thought. 'I couldn't be with her all the time. Now, how different life is for her. If only we'd come to Granny at once! But one is so helpless when one is young. And there was Daddy's will – which he would never have made if he had

68

known Aunt Ethel better.'

She wrenched her thoughts away from this unlikeable relative, undressed and slipped into bed in that strong, silvery light without waking Josie.

There were other people to think of, far more important figures now in her life. That rather odd conversation between her grandmother and David! There was an underlying meaning there – but what? Was David planning to marry Delphine, and so, eventually, bring her into the management side of the hotel? If so, did Granny really suppose she could thwart him indefinitely?

She knew his value. Her hard common sense would prevent her sacking him if he chose to disregard her wishes and make Delphine his wife. Surely in the clash of wills David would eventually prove the winner, owning and running the Hermes with Delphine's help. He would be generous, of course – and come to that, Mrs. Vassilou was quite capable of looking after her own interests.

Things would work out, probably, with his former employer – or senior partner, as Granny styled herself when in a good mood – living in comfortable retirement.

'And Josie and I would be with her,' she thought. 'I'd find a job quite easily. I might even forget darling Guy one day, and marry someone here, though it's most unlikely.'

And with that sober reflection she, too, fell asleep.

CHAPTER FOUR

After the usual pleasant and peaceful breakfast, served early, as always, she left Josie ostensibly helping her grandmother before going to Miss Taylor's class, and went over to the main part of the hotel.

The routine which her grandmother had planned for her – pretty loosely, so far – took her first to the office. And this, because it entailed an encounter with Delphine, was something which she was glad to get over right away.

'I *must* try to get on with this tiresome woman,' she thought. 'Surely there's some way of breaking down her hostility.'

But when she wished her a friendly good morning, and asked politely if there were any personal letters for her grandmother, she was greeted with a curt, 'No! One for you, though.' And at the same time a bulky envelope was thrust into her hand.

It bore an English stamp, and for a moment the notion rushed into her mind that Guy had somehow found her address, and was writing to say— But before her thoughts could move a step further, she saw that the handwriting on the envelope was Aunt Ethel's, and she turned away in sick disappointment, cramming the unwanted letter into a pocket of her spotless white overall. She was in no hurry to read it. Never had she known Aunt Ethel the bearer of pleasant news. But, absurdly, it seemed a heavy weight, as she carried it around, and she knew that as soon as she had got through her usual tasks she would have to look for a quiet spot and see what it contained.

To her deep satisfaction Nicos was all smiles. The quarrel with Chef over the Kyria's supper tray was, it seemed, forgotten. What was important was that the family conclave over the possession of certain olive-trees had gone off satisfactorily.

'This brother-in-law of mine,' and he gestured with his thumb towards the kitchen quarters, 'is a fine man of business – and mathematician! Even with all the noise and arguments going on he was able in little more than three hours to work things out.' He smiled with satisfaction, as he added: 'And he had the sense to see that I got my rights.'

'That's good, Nicos. And how many olive trees were involved?'

'Two. And very good ones,' he told her proudly. 'Of course there are a great many of us to share – living all over the island. Sixty-three, Chef reckoned. But fair treatment, that's the thing, all part of our Greek heritage of independence.'

And then, as she left Nicos to his cheerful reflections and went to take a look at the other public rooms, she ran into Miss Taylor, carrying some books and papers, and looking decidedly less poised and placid than usual.

'How I can be expected to teach when I'm bothered with a lot of nonsense, I don't know,' she exclaimed with quiet vehemence. 'Your grandmother rings up to tell me that Theo is hanging around there, wanting to come to my class with Josie. I say, "Of course, let the child come". And then this tiresome Delphine says, "No, thank you. Theo is on holiday. He must come and play on my balcony".'

'I don't see what you can do about it,' Irene murmured, thankful that the only occupants of the writing-room were, at that moment, some deaf old ladies.

'I suppose not. But I shall certainly tell Kyria Vassilou that Delphine was most ungracious to me. Did she think I should charge a fee for having her child in my class for a few odd mornings?'

Irene shrugged her shoulders. 'She's not exactly polite to me,' she observed. 'And I can't do anything about that, either.'

The incident went out of her head. After all, it was characteristic of Delphine to show this crazy possessiveness over Theo – a possessiveness with very little evidence of warm affection.

Her own concern was to have these lovely reception rooms looking their best – doing the flowers was in itself a long business – and then settle down to read this unwanted and unwelcome letter.

With a large group of tourists leaving, and another expected, endless little jobs turned up – and continued to do so all day. And it wasn't until siesta time that she had a few minutes to herself. Then, lying out in a long chair on the bedroom veranda, Josie asleep indoors in her bed, she tore open the envelope.

'Dear Irene,' Aunt Ethel wrote, on the cheap, lined

paper she always used for letters to people she styled unimportant. 'We hope that you and Josie are well, which is more than your uncle and I am in this trying weather. Not that this will interest you. However, the reason for this letter is to tell you that we are going to have this house turned into two flats, as we had planned to do years ago before your uncle decided that it was our duty to give a home to you and Josie, and dropped the idea.

In spite of all we have done for you, we are not asking for financial help towards the now much higher costs of conversion, only payment for redecorating the bedroom you occupied, which will now serve as sitting-room in the upper flat. I enclose the builders' estimate for the work.

By the way, when tidying up recently I came across a book with your friend Guy Cosway's name in it: a volume of poetry which had fallen behind a bookshelf. As you never chose to give me his private address, I sent it to your old office. He wrote back so nicely, I wouldn't be surprised if we saw that big Bentley of his drawing up outside the house again, one of these days. If he does drop in, is there any message for the poor fellow? You treated him very badly, and very foolishly, in our opinion.

Yrs.,

Ethel Meredith'

Confused, angry, and apprehensive, too, Irene pulled out another folded sheet from the envelope – the estimate from a Maida Vale builder which included costs not only for redecorating that bedroom which she and Josie had occupied for those none-too-happy years in London, but for new, modern windows, repairs to floorboards, and even for providing extra electric points.

The total sum shocked her. Reasonable it might be, from the builders' point of view. But, as Aunt Ethel must surely know, she simply did not possess that much money.

Did Aunt Ethel imagine that she was going to meet this preposterous demand by applying to her grandmother? If so, she would quickly find herself mistaken. To submit to any such calls would mean becoming involved in something very near blackmail. Moreover, she couldn't believe for a moment that Uncle Herbert had any part or say in the matter. He had always maintained, in the face of Aunt Ethel's angry assertions to the contrary, that by the terms of his brother's will the pair of them had received generous financial treatment for giving a home to their orphaned nieces. It was unbelievable that he should try to extract money from them now, even if there was justice in the claim.

She thrust the envelope and its contents into one of her drawers, under a pile of handkerchiefs. She didn't want Josie's sharp eyes noticing Aunt Ethel's crabbed handwriting; didn't want the stream of agitated questions which would certainly follow any attempts at evasion.

The slight sound of the drawer being closed was enough to awake Josie, who stretched her arms, slid out of bed and announced happily: 'Theo's coming over to play in our shed. It's Granny's idea, so that tiresome mother of his can't say no.'

'You mustn't make snide remarks about Mrs. Cipriani,' Irene told her reprovingly. 'Apart from getting you into trouble sooner or later – no grown-ups like children to be cheeky – it's unfair. It's sad to be a widow. She feels that Theo's all she's got, that's why she clings to him.'

Josie looked unconvinced. 'You've told me lots of times that if you really love people you want them to be happy. Why does Mrs. Cipriani stop Theo doing nice things, like coming out for a drive with Mr. Nikolaides?'

'Darling, I don't know. But you must accept that it's not your business or mine, and keep that little mouth of yours shut.'

'O.K.' But the child's tone was almost petulant, and Irene thought suddenly: 'I used to worry about her being too malleable. It's only right and healthy that she should be a bit of a rebel sometimes.'

All the same she was relieved when Theo's voice, calling 'Ho, Jo!' from the garden, gave a fresh direction to the little girl's thoughts. She pulled on her jeans – her grandmother had ordered some for both children – and ran out to the balcony, calling out in fluent Greek that she was just coming, and was out of the room and sliding down the well-polished banisters in a matter of seconds.

Left to herself in this abrupt fashion – and how good it was that Josie was losing her clinging ways – Irene strolled over to the office.

Delphine had grudgingly consented to David's suggestion that she should hand over the filing to the newcomer – and so relieve herself of some of the donkeywork. She knew well enough that it was Mrs. Vassilou who was behind the idea, seeing in it a means whereby her granddaughter would acquire valuable knowledge of the working of the hotel, knew that opposition would be useless. All she could do was to discourage Irene from asking her help and advice with any problems that arose, and in this she was adept.

On this occasion she was absent from the office, and David had taken her place at the desk – free, for the moment, from the constant demands and queries of guests and staff.

'I was hoping you'd turn up,' he said. 'Delphine's lying down with a headache. I'm sorry for her, poor girl. But it does give me a chance of having a little talk with you.'

His voice, though courteous, was not particularly cordial, and Irene at once began to wonder what she had done wrong – what mistake she had made. She was very soon to learn.

Talking to her rather as a child, Irene thought, David asked her if she couldn't behave a little more tactfully to Delphine.

'But I fell backwards trying to keep the peace,' Irene protested, flushing with indignation. 'If you knew how rude she was to me!'

'I'm sure she doesn't mean it, Irene. She's a bundle of nerves, these days.'

74

'Well, what am I supposed to have done?' Irene demanded, with a touch, though she did not realize it, of her grandmother's *hauteur*.

'She didn't like your telling Colonel Bykers to complain to me about some mistake Delphine had made in his fortnightly bill. Why couldn't you mention it to her yourself, Irene, in a friendly way?'

'Because I'm pretty sure she was doing it to annoy the old boy, whom she makes no secret of disliking. You know as well as I do that she's neither careless nor stupid – and he had pointed out the mistake to her more than once.'

'I know she disagreed with your grandmother giving that couple special terms.' David spoke stiffly. 'At the same time I can hardly credit that she would dare show her resentment in such a ridiculous fashion.'

Irene, her temper rising, shrugged her shoulders. 'And the next complaint?' she demanded. 'Is she still moaning because I was a little late coming in from that drive with Andreas Nikolaides?'

'Actually she was very sporting about it, didn't in the least mind taking on your jobs as well as her own. What she did resent was your interfering in a staff quarrel, when she'd particularly asked you to keep out of it. She says, and I must say I agree, that you have to know the people of any country very well – and possess an intimate knowledge of their language – to intervene in their disputes.'

Her eyes met his in a glance as steady as his own.

'If I hadn't happened to walk straight into the row, and persuaded both Nicos and Chef to use a bit of common sense, you and my grandmother might have gone without supper last night,' she told him. And then she added, her dark head held high: 'Even if you happen to be in love with Delphine, and object to my coming here, you ought to behave with common justice. As it is, you're grossly unfair. But you're not going to drive me out!'

A succession of newly arrived guests came drifting along then – to be greeted, and offered helpful information. The hall porter and pages, too, carrying suitcases, and asking for instructions. All was bustle and excitement.

It was minutes later, after both had been called away, but were now back in the office again, that David echoed Irene's phrase – and with sharp impatience.

'Drive you out!' he exclaimed. 'Really, Irene, how dramatic can you get? Just because I ask you to exercise a little tact towards a woman, older than yourself, who has had a raw deal from life, you go up in the air like a rocket. If you'd known what it was to suffer as she has done – to bring that child up on her own—'

'How do you know that I haven't suffered?' she demanded. 'Just because I'm young—'

'I'm sorry, that was clumsy of me. But will you please believe me when I say I've come to regard you as an asset here, and so sensible that I can't understand your going off the handle over poor Delphine.'

She shrugged her shoulders. 'I don't see her in the same light as you do.' She had noticed that he had made no denial of being in love with the older woman. But hurriedly she added: 'I admit I'm in a prickly mood today. I've had a disturbing letter from London.'

'From someone who matters a lot to you?' His voice had become gentler.

For a second she hesitated, then said firmly: 'No. This Aunt Ethel, who's such an obsession with Josie, is worrying me over a business matter.'

His face cleared. 'Maybe I could help you.' Then, as a couple of perplexed-looking guests bore down on them, he added under his breath: 'Come over here around nine if you'd like to consult me. Most of the guests will be watching the film show then, and we should get a little privacy. If you don't come, I shall quite understand.'

And with that he went forward to settle still another problem, and left her to her filing and to any other odd jobs that might arise.

Siesta time well over now, even for one or two ancient residents, who were apt to stretch it out, she had even more interruptions, but nothing to put her seriously out of her stride.

The visitors were, for the most part, thoroughly appreciative, both of the amenities of the hotel, and of the beauties of 'Aphrodite's Home' as, in their various languages they knew this island of Cyprus. They liked to linger for a friendly chat, to describe what they had seen and heard, to outline the tours they planned to make. The elderly residents, too, enjoyed a word with her. With her genuine liking for people and interest in them, Irene found pleasure in these little chats. She knew that this delighted her grandmother, who in an almost uncanny way was aware of all that went on in the hotel, but despite Delphine's sarcasm, she had no ulterior motives for her behaviour.

Trivial interruptions should be politely discouraged – that was Delphine's idea. They held up the efficient working of the hotel, might cause serious mistakes. And, so Irene believed, David was more than a little inclined to agree with her.

Reflecting, she could see that her grandmother was right in refusing to give Delphine the hope of entering even into joint management with David. She might make him an admirable wife, she told herself. But as a business partner, with power in her hands, she would be a disaster.

As she came to some correspondence from Sweden – Cyprus had many devotees in the Scandinavian countries – she recalled sharply that incident which was never very far from the surface of her mind. She had been saying to herself just now that her grandmother knew all that passed in her beloved Hotel Hermes. She didn't, of course. What on earth would her reaction be if she knew of Delphine's destruction of that letter from Stockholm? She would have forgiven Delphine for forgetting to note the contents. Anyone could make a mistake. But to tear it up, pretend it had never come – that would have been another matter.

'What made Delphine think I wouldn't split on her?' Irene wondered, as many times before. And always the same answer came: 'Because she knows David would take her word against mine – and even, perhaps, persuade Granny to do the same—'

No! She couldn't believe that her grandmother would distrust her, whatever Delphine might think. But from every point of view, she felt sure, she had done right to keep silence.

If the hotel was to continue its prosperous course, there must be at least a surface peace within its borders.

Finishing the filing, she went into the dining-room, for her usual last-minute tour of the tables, and found Nicos' young cousin, Panos, gloomily preparing a tray.

'What's the matter?' she asked him, for he was usually cheerful enough.

'Kyria Cipriani is to have her dinner in her room,' he said sulkily.

'Well, what about it? You often take trays upstairs, now Nicos finds you manage so well.'

'Whatever I take her will be wrong,' the boy declared. 'She has a spite against me, that one, just because I stand up for myself when she accuses me of doing careless and stupid things which I have not done at all.'

'Are you sure you're not rude to her?' Irene suggested mildly, careful to conceal the sympathy she felt. 'What have you been saying to her?'

His dark head went up, and his eyes flashed.

'I say: "Kyria Cipriani, you are not my boss. I obey Nicos, Kyria Vassilou—" ' he ticked off the names on his fingers – 'Mees Irene and Kyrie David. Not you?'

'It's much better to say nothing and look polite,' Irene advised him, trying not to smile. 'If you carry the tray up with that scowl, you're certain to get black looks.'

'If I carried it right to her door, would you take it in?' he pleaded. 'Nicos would agree. He thinks you are wonderful!'

She shook her head. 'I don't think it would do at all,' she said, reflecting that her reception would probably be far worse than this young man's.

78

He shrugged his shoulders. 'She means to get me the sack,' he said. 'Because I happen to know something about her which other people don't – something which I have every intention of keeping to myself, as a man of honour, brought up, moreover in Greece itself!'

Fortunately Nicos came in just then, to eye his young relative with impatience, and to exclaim: 'Still boasting about having lived in Greece – boring poor Mees Irene with your nonsense!' Then, catching sight of the tray prepared for Delphine, he continued irritably: 'I'd better take it up myself when Chef serves dinner. What with your tactlessness, and her fussy ways—'

It was a relief to Irene as well as to Panos that Nicos was taking over the unwelcome task. She hated the idea of getting mixed up in these silly little quarrels and intrigues, particularly when Delphine was involved.

Not for a moment did she believe that the boy knew anything to Delphine's discredit. It was just a theatrical gesture made by a temperamental teenager. But how carefully one had to walk in this fantastically beautiful island of Cyprus.

While she was considering, as she sipped her sherry that evening in her grandmother's sitting-room, whether or not she would confide in David, something happened to startle her. Mrs. Vassilou up in her bedroom dressing for dinner – though her clothes, invariably black, were simple, she kept up a certain style – Irene found herself alone with Josie.

The child, usually absorbed at these odd moments in one of her grandmother's jig-saws, kept sending her odd glances, and at last Irene asked her quietly if anything was the matter.

'Oh, no.' Josie's manner was unnaturally offhand. 'I was only wondering if the letter you were reading on the balcony this afternoon was from Aunt Ethel.'

'It was. But what made you think so?'

'Theo told me that a letter came for you yesterday with an English stamp. He saw it on his mother's desk, and asked her for it – the stamp, I mean. She was cross, told him to mind his own business, and not to ask you for it.'

'He can have it, of course!' Irene was thinking indignantly: 'Yesterday? Theo saw it yesterday? How dare Delphine delay my letters?'

But her mind switched back quickly to Josie.

'Does she want us to go back?' the child was asking, her blue eyes huge in her small white face. 'Could she make us?'

'Certainly not, you little donkey! Far from wanting us, she's having the house made into two flats, so that she and Uncle Herbert can get money for rent.'

Josie relaxed, like a wilting flower put in water. But she was still frowning a little as she demanded: 'If there wasn't something – something awful – in that letter, why did you hide it in your drawer? I couldn't help seeing you do it, out of the corner of my eye, and – don't be angry with me, Irene, I very nearly got it out and read it, only I thought it might be a love letter from Guy.'

'Darling, you know as well as I do that you must *never* read other people's letters. So I'm not going to say any more about that. But what's happened to your knowledge that you could always trust me? I haven't changed.'

For answer Josie flung herself into her sister's arms.

'Mrs. Cipriani says things to the visitors sometimes. Theo heard her tell a lady who wanted to see you to say good-bye that you were too busy to come to the office – and that anyway you probably wouldn't be here when she came next year because you'd be going back to England.'

'That, my darling, is sheer nonsense,' Irene declared, hugging her. 'It's what's called wishful thinking. I'll explain about it some time. As for Aunt Ethel's letter, she wants me to send her some money to pay for the work on the flats. And I'm not going to.'

'Of *course* not!' Josie was highly indignant.

She jumped up, and running over to her grandmother's desk, rattled a china pig that was becoming mysteriously fuller each week.

'Neither am I,' she said severely as she brandished it – then grinned gappily at her own absurdity – a tiny incident, but it gave a lift to Irene's heart. For the first time ever Josie was referring to Aunt Ethel, not only without fear but with actual amusement. She was finding her ridiculous. In that way, surely, healing must come.

Mrs. Vassilou came down just then, regal as ever with her silver hair piled high, but her classic features lit up with pleasure at the sight of her granddaughters waiting there for her.

'My darlings, how happy it makes me to have you living here with me.' It was not the first time she had said this, but always her words held a deep sincerity. 'You give me a sense of home in a way I've never had since your dear grandfather died.'

'All I wish now is that we'd come to you years ago,' Irene told her.

'Yes!' Josie nodded vigorously. 'We ought to have saved up hard and run away. I used to make up plans, sometimes, after Irene had been telling me things about you – and about Cyprus – ! About collecting and hiding food and blankets – and pocket-money, of course – and stowing away in a Canal barge which would get us to the sea, and a cargo ship—'

Her grandmother smiled. 'You've an inventive mind, my child. But now here's someone bringing over our dinner. Say grace for us, and we'll sit down.'

Carefully Josie crossed herself, in the Greek-Orthodox way her grandmother had taught her, and they sat down to the excellent meal of stuffed vine leaves and fresh vegetables which Chef had sent over for them.

Relaxed now, Irene gave up the idea of consulting David, or anyone else, about her aunt's insolent demands. He might very well advise her to let a solicitor handle the matter, but because of Uncle Herbert, this was something she would not do. Uncle Herbert, she felt pretty certain, would know nothing of his wife's suggestion: the arrival of a lawyer's letter would shock him to the core. No. She would do what common sense dictated: write to Aunt

Ethel and state definitely that she did not possess the amount of money requested, and while she wished her well with her scheme of conversion, could give her no financial help whatever with it.

All the same it would be discourteous, she felt, not to go across later in the evening, and explain to him that she had sorted out the matter for herself. It had been kind of him to offer his help.

She found him waiting for her, not in the office but in the entrance hall.

'Everything's in order,' he said casually, 'with Hercules around to answer the telephone. So what about a very short run in the car? Ten minutes or so, along the sea road.'

'I'd like that. But, David, I shan't need to ask your advice about that worrying letter. I've worked things out for myself.'

He smiled. 'There speaks Kyria Vassilou's granddaughter!' They passed out together through the swing doors by which she had just entered. 'You know, my dear, I can well envisage you in days to come in supreme command at the Hermes. You might even marry a Vassilou cousin as a kind of Prince Consort. There are enough of them in the island.'

'For a dour Scot you seem prone to flights of romantic fancy,' she countered coolly, as they reached the waiting car, parked round a corner of the building.

'Marriages in Cyprus aren't invariably love matches.' He handed her into the car, and took his seat beside her. 'Material considerations have a certain importance, as in other Continental countries.'

With Aunt Ethel's references to Guy Cosway burning in her brain, she said shortly: 'I'm in no mind to marry anyone, for any reason. It's old-fashioned to think that a woman can't choose to stay single.'

'Or that if she does, she will rule out lovers!' His reply came pat.

She flung him an impatient glance.

'What's got into you tonight, David?'

'Maybe the scent of orange blossom mixed up with the tang of the sea!' He was smiling now. 'After being cooped up all day, making oneself pleasant to visitors, it has its effect.'

She made no comment, nor did he seem to expect one; he was looking away from her and through the open car window. Presently, as they went along the rough, almost deserted shore road, he stopped the car.

'Let's get out for a minute or two,' he said. 'And tell me if you've ever seen anything so beautiful as the moon sending that silver path over the dark, quiet sea – anything so exquisite as the sapphire radiance of that cloudless sky.'

'Never except in Cyprus,' she told him. 'You must remember that for years this island was my home.'

'I do forget it sometimes, when you're in a downright British mood,' he admitted.

She laughed then. 'Just as I forget your Cypriot blood when the MacLeod temperament is uppermost – as it usually is.'

'But the Scottish isles are lovely, too. I could live happily in Barra or tiny Eriskay. With the right person.'

'And a good strong mackintosh!' she gibed.

He gave her an odd glance. 'What an aggravating, prickly creature you are! I don't know why I like you at all.'

'I didn't know you did!' She could have bitten back the words next minute. For wouldn't he think she was encouraging him in this tiresome mood of sentimental nonsense?

She needn't have been afraid.

'Well, isn't that the world's wonder?' he declaimed to the surrounding silence. 'The competent Miss Meredith admits that there's something she doesn't know.'

'And in this case doesn't believe,' she returned loftily. 'Now, thank you for the drive, but what about getting home?'

'High time. Our ten minutes have stretched into twenty.'

He drove her straight back to her grandmother's door, dropped her there, and with the most formal 'Good night' went on his way.

She explained to her grandmother at once where she had been, half afraid of a mild rebuke for unconventional behaviour, but nothing of the kind was forthcoming.

'A few minutes in the fresh air would do you good,' was all the old lady had to say.

Indeed next day, Delphine being on duty again, she invited him over for a drink before dinner, together with a few old friends, from Kyrenia and the neighbourhood.

She had intended to ask Miss Taylor, but she, it seemed, was otherwise engaged. She was entertaining Josie and Theo in her room, giving them an out-of-class lesson in making toys from bits and pieces for young patients in hospital – a circumstance which pleased Irene, who was English enough to feel that children were out of place in a sherry party.

She dressed for this minor festivity in green leaf-patterned chiffon, simply cut. It had been a favourite with Guy and, because of this, she had been tempted to get rid of it before leaving England. But with little money to spend on her Cyprus outfit, she had decided to put sentiment aside and bring it with her. She couldn't really afford to discard one of the most expensive and becoming dresses in her somewhat meagre wardrobe.

Her grandmother was quick to show her appreciation of the trouble she had taken with her appearance.

'You're as beautiful as your dear mother,' she declared, a sentiment which was repeated in nearly the same words by the old friends to whom she proudly introduced her granddaughter.

Among the older folk was a sprinkling of younger relatives, including – and this amused Irene – two good-looking Vassilou cousins. But if David, too, was amused – remembering his words of the previous evening – he did not show it. Some time passed before he found himself alone with her, and then he was in his normal matter-of-fact mood.

There had been some general conversation about the little Irene had yet seen of the island – about the beauty spots she had almost a duty to visit – and now he said amiably: 'I'm trying to plan taking you and Josie to Limassol to visit my parents, but it's a very long trip. We must wait until the tourist stream slackens. But there's a short trip I could manage, to a place I love, and which you and Josie too should see. The village and Abbey of Bella Pais.'

Her eyes shone.

'It's one of the places I best remember! That lovely garden in the ruins. The Tree of Idleness in the village square. Why, there might still be people up there who remember me and my parents. Please let's go!'

He smiled at her enthusiasm. 'We'll try to make it next week – or better still, the week after. We look like having a lull then. But I mustn't monopolize you. Here's young Nick Vassilou coming.'

She raised a quizzical eyebrow. 'One of my eligible cousins?'

'Definitely,' was his light reply. 'But don't let him whisk you to Bella Pais, that's all I ask. My invitation came first – and fair's fair.'

She enjoyed the little party, more than previous small social gatherings which her grandmother had arranged for her, because she was now fluent in Greek, seldom having to stop to search for a word. Everyone, she felt, liked her and wanted her to feel at home in their breathtakingly beautiful island. And so she would in time, she thought, when once those memories of Guy, and their happy times together, faded away – like the colours of some old forgotten painting.

Late that evening, the party over, and her last-minute jobs at the hotel completed, she was sitting quietly with her grandmother, when the telephone rang and, answering it, she heard Andreas Nikolaides' voice. Guests at the sherry party had been talking about a new night club that

85

was shortly to be opened in Nicosia, and now she had a sharp reminder. Andreas wanted to be first in the field with an invitation to her to accompany him to what he called the inauguration night. Everything would be in order, he said, before she had time to demur. His young sister and her husband would be coming from Larnaca to stay the night and attend the function. And probably some friends would join their party. There would be no question at all of upsetting her grandmother by suggesting an evening *à deux*.

'I must consult her all the same,' she told him firmly, 'and choose the right moment for doing it.'

He gave that lazy laugh of his. 'Naturally. But don't forget, I asked you first. You'll get other invitations for sure. It's a big event.'

She said nothing to her grandmother just then, beyond that Andreas was hoping she would go out with him again some time.

She wasn't quite sure that she wanted to accept this invitation. Why, she didn't quite know. Was it that although she found Andreas a gay and amusing companion and, with his undeniable good looks, an enviable escort, she had certain reservations about him?

Anyway, she was not going to decide all in a minute. The Club wasn't opening until at least a month. She had plenty of time to make up her mind.

Things went reasonably smoothly for the next few days with David firmly back in his polite but impersonal mood.

'I don't know why I like you!' Had he really said that, when they were standing looking at the moonlit sea? Said it in a tone he had never used to her before? She could hardly believe it.

This was his real everyday self – the man who, praising her occasionally, was far more likely to find fault with her for minor mistakes, explaining coolly that it was part of her training, that Kyria Vassilou had emphasized that he must take trouble with her, see that she learnt all the ins and outs of the business.

'Then I must be grateful to you,' was her philosophical response. 'But I wish you would lay off when Delphine's around. That supercilious smile of hers—!'

'And I wish you'd lay off Delphine! She can't do a thing right, so far as you're concerned.' His voice was impatient.

She flared up at that. 'Sentimental Scot!' she jeered. 'I could say a lot more – about people who are as blind as bats. But I won't!'

'Thank goodness for that,' he said icily. 'And now will you explain why you've told Nicos to move those English spinsters to a better table? They're paying less than anyone.'

'Because Miss Mildred, the older one, has trouble with her eyes,' she returned shortly. 'There's less glare where she's sitting now. The couple they've changed with can't have enough sunshine.'

'Like your grandmother, you've an answer for everything,' he told her irritably. 'And you're just as prejudiced, too.'

'If I've got my knife into Delphine – which is what he means – it's entirely her fault,' she thought rebelliously, as he left her to think out a new flower arrangement for the dining-room.

But she had to admit that the older woman was making far less effort now to prevent Theo and Josie playing together. Beyond remarking occasionally that she wished her son had a boy to run around with – one of his own age, moreover, instead of a girl older than himself – she made no move to separate them. And every afternoon now they played happily together in the old shed – cleaned certainly, but not over-tidied, and because of its semi-seclusion, still living up to their description of 'our secret place'.

And then, without warning, Delphine uttered her ultimatum. Theo wasn't learning enough with Miss Taylor, whose class was really for foreign children. He must go back to Kyrenia, to the school he had been attending

87

before. Far from making any difficulty, the school author-
ities were expecting him to return, and she was arranging
with her mother to take him home to her at once.

Although it was undeniable that Delphine was perfectly in the right, the suddenness of her decision, and the
consequent distress of the children, lessened any sympathy that might have been felt for her. Just why the
children had found such happiness in their companionship, no one quite knew. Each, evidently had qualities that appealed to the other, making the difference in
age unimportant. Where, in their place, grown-ups would
have known that a parting was inevitable, and not very
far ahead, they had lived in the happy moment.

'You must bring him here for week-ends – and more
frequently than you used to,' Mrs. Vassilou told Delphine, heading the little group which had gathered round
David's car to bid Theo good-bye.

'It's very kind of you, but I think it's a little unsettling,
leaving his home so much. However, we'll see.'

Theo, sitting alone at the back, made no comment. He
looked neither to the left nor the right as the car drove
off. His male pride was asserting itself. He was determined not to cry.

Josie made no bones about showing her emotion. She
burst into tears. There was a rush to comfort her, but
Irene resolutely bore her away to their own room. In
Maida Vale Josie had been unnaturally stoical. Here, surrounded with affection, and over-indulged, there was a
danger of her becoming spoiled – soft even! And she told
her gently but firmly that if Theo could put on a brave
front – a little boy of six – so could she. There were children in Miss Taylor's class whom she could play with.
Granny would surely let her ask some of them up to
tea.

Josie dabbed her eyes with the handkerchief which
Irene had lent her.

'Well, I shan't take them to our secret place,' she declared stubbornly. 'Even if Theo never comes back.'

'Of course he will. You must try to be sensible, darling.

Mrs. Cipriani is quite right about sending him back to the Kyrenia school. This has been a kind of holiday for him, and he'll be back for others.'

Josie shrugged her shoulders. The tears were dying away, but her small face was mutinous.

'She might have given us a day's warning,' she said. 'We had some lovely plans for a game we were playing. She's a very horrid woman, almost as bad as Aunt Ethel!'

'Now stop it, darling. Chef wants some specially good lemons for dinner tonight. We'll go and look for some in the orchard.'

If she had been seriously afraid that her little sister was getting too much pampering, her apprehensions would have increased when David returned some hours later bringing back not only Delphine but a large basket labelled 'Miss Josephine Meredith'.

He dropped Delphine at the main entrance, and came across to where Irene and Josie were sitting on a bench near their grandmother's front door, poring over a book of Cyprus birds.

'Hullo, Irene! Hi, Niobe!' he called out.

Josie jumped up and ran to meet him.

'Who's Niobe? And what have you got in that basket?'

'The first answer is that she was a Greek lady, said to be "all tears" – as you were when I took Theo away this morning. In the basket is another friend to play with.' He knelt down and raised the lid. 'You won't be lonesome and weepy with this chap around.' And out jumped an exuberant puppy who fell on Josie with delight, wagging his tail, and barking and licking her hands in an ecstasy of delight.

'He's *beautiful*!' she exclaimed. And indeed he was – a pale-gold, silky creature, resembling a golden retriever, but smaller and slimmer. 'I've seen several about since I came to Cyprus.'

'An aristocrat, if ever there was one!' He was favouring

Irene with his attentions now.

David smiled across at her. 'Very much so. The Crusaders brought the breed here from Western Europe. You see them in old paintings. How they've kept the strain pure, I can't imagine.'

'Has he got a name?' Josie demanded.

'He has, indeed, and a very fine one. Guy! After the famous and valiant knight, Guy de Lusignan, whom you've probably learnt about in Miss Taylor's Cyprus History class.'

'Oh, we couldn't call him *Guy*!' Josie, dismayed, looked from David to Irene, who had gone pink with embarrassment. 'Not *possibly*!'

David, taken aback, recovered himself quickly.

'Call him what you please, kid. Do you like him? – that's the main thing.'

'I think he's adorable,' Josie exclaimed. She ran up to the big man and threw her arms round his waist. 'And there's another thing I think – that you're the kindest man in the world!'

He laughed. 'No other woman has paid me such a compliment.' He swung her up into his arms. 'Are you going to give me a kiss?'

'Several!' And she suited her action to her words. 'I'm going to call you Uncle David, too.'

'Thank you, niece Josie. And now,' he set her on her feet, 'mind you look after your dog. The people I bought him from have sent a list of instructions about his food and so on. He's house-trained, by the way, but keep an eye on him until he's settled down.'

'I suppose Granny won't object?' For a moment Irene was concerned.

He shook his head. 'I told her before I took Delphine and Theo to Kyrenia today that I wanted to give Josie a cheer-up present. She agreed with me that nothing could be more suitable. And what do you think? I bought his brother for Theo.'

'Did Mrs. Cipriani mind?' Josie sounded positively alarmed.

David gave her a sharp look. 'Why should you think that? Of course she didn't.'

'What did she say?' Josie persisted.

'Josie, shut up! Don't ask impertinent questions!' Irene was wondering what on earth the child would say next.

'It's all right, my dears.' David was coolly amiable again. 'She didn't tell me I was the kindest man she had ever met – but she said some very nice things indeed!' He looked across at Irene. 'She's all set to catch up with what she calls the backlog caused by having Theo here – though I think her strong sense of duty makes her exaggerate. However, that being so, and there being a gap of a day or two between a crowd leaving, and another arriving, what about letting me drive you tomorrow to one of my favourite places – Bella Pais?'

Josie, Irene reflected next moment, had certainly changed a great deal from the quiet repressed child of those Maida Vale days.

'We'd love to, wouldn't we, Irene?' she cried eagerly. 'You and me, and my puppy. We'll have found a name for him by then.'

David looked again at Irene inquiringly.

'Yes, please,' she said.

Mrs. Vassilou came over just then. Since her granddaughters' arrival in Cyprus she had been spending less time over at the hotel, rejoicing in the homelike atmosphere they created, but now she was beginning to take up the threads again, much to the satisfaction of her guests.

She approved of the puppy – but Josie must train him not to jump up and damage people's clothes.

'In your dear grandfather's time we always had a dog – one just like this. You remember him, Irene?'

'I do, indeed, now I look back. Lance – wasn't that his name?'

Mrs. Vassilou nodded.

'And I gather from Delphine, who went with David to buy him, that Josie's new pet is called Guy!'

'Oh, we're going to choose another name, Granny,' Josie piped up. 'What about Prince?'

The old lady looked faintly surprised, but made no comment.

'We must go shopping for him,' she told the child. 'He'll need a collar and lead and a basket to sleep in—'

'And a squeaky rubber toy!' Josie's face was alight. 'When we were living in London, a girl at school had one for her peke. It was glorious fun. I used to nip into her house on my way back from school. Aunt Ethel never knew.'

'This Aunt Ethel – surely she did something else than get cross with you, Josie!' Mrs. Vassilou's tone was faintly reproving.

'Yes, she went in for competitions.' Josie's reply came pat.

'What competition?'

'From advertisements in the papers and on packets from the stores. She won quite a few small prizes. Nothing big, though. It was because of its being a fiddle, she said, that she never won anything really decent. But she always went on trying for a car or a washing machine or a new TV set.'

'Then she has one great virtue – perseverance. An admirable quality, my dear. Though with her talent for disapproval, I'm surprised she should have chosen such a sporting hobby.'

With the puppy shut away in the kitchen, and only emitting an occasional howl, the three of them sat down to lunch, and Irene told her grandmother of David's invitation.

'Of course, let him take you to Bella Pais by all means. It's one of my own special places. When no child came along to us, your grandfather and I used to go to the little church there and pray to Our Lady for a baby – and she sent us your dear mother.'

'Oh, Granny, won't you come, too?' Josie exclaimed. 'You could sit in front, and Irene and I and the puppy behind.'

'My darling, it's sweet of you, but that would mean leaving Delphine alone, and she hasn't seemed quite herself the last two or three months. For one or two reasons I'd rather be around.'

'Should she see a doctor?' Irene ventured.

'I wish she would. But she's stubborn. Nerves are her trouble, I think.'

Irene said no more just then, but later that day, when Josie was in bed and asleep, she raised the subject again.

'It seems to me that Delphine's nervousness dates from my arrival here,' she said unhappily. 'She feels, I suppose, that I'm supplanting her – and that upsets her.'

'Then she should talk things out with me,' Mrs. Vassilou said firmly. 'The very fact that she's so temperamental makes it obvious that she should not expect to manage a hotel – ever! In a more subordinate role she is – or could be – excellent. If she decided to leave the Hermes I'd give her a splendid reference, and I'm certain she could find a fine job, either here or in Greece, where she's spent several years.' And then she added, shaking her silver head: 'She's jealous of you, no doubt, but not only in regard to her position here. David, who resented your coming to the Hermes at first, is beginning to like you more than quite pleases her.'

'I don't see much sign of that myself, Granny!' Far from showing embarrassment, Irene was ironically amused at the idea. 'He may be finding me a little more competent than he expected – not quite such an ignorant fool—'

'My dear, he's never thought that of you.' Mrs. Vassilou was indignant, bristling at the very idea. 'As if my granddaughter – well educated, and holding an important post in London—!'

'Not all that important,' Irene protested. 'I happen to be good at languages, that's all. Anyway, I very rarely draw a word of praise from David. As for anything warmer, that's just a good joke. And what do I care!'

'Are you still grieving over that man in England?' her

grandmother asked her suddenly. 'Guy – I imagine that's his name!'

Irene was startled at that, then said, with a shrug of her shoulders: 'I suppose everyone will suspect now that there's a special person in England caled Guy. Josie made that obvious. So there is, but I'm doing my best to forget him.'

'And is he forgetting you, my darling?' The old lady was looking at her in a troubled sort of way.

'Unfortunately not, judging from Aunt Ethel's last letter to me. He thinks me obstinate and cruel – which is precisely what I think of him.'

Mrs. Vassilou continued to look anxious. 'If you were to compose your differences, would he be content to work over here in Cyprus?' she asked. 'I must not be selfish, but the thought of you and Josie leaving me and returning to live all those thousands of miles away strikes cold on my heart. It's such joy to have you.' The tears came to her dark eyes, and she brushed them away. 'There now, I shouldn't have said that. I *am* selfish. It shames me. I'm an old woman, with most of my life gone. You have all before you. Your happiness, that's what counts.'

Irene ran across to her, folded her in her strong young arms.

'From the very day we came here, you've surrounded us with love, made us feel we belong, just as our parents did. This is our home, and here we stay.'

But Mrs. Vassilou had recovered herself now; the moment of weakness gone, she was poised and dignified as ever, releasing herself gently from Irene's embrace.

'My darling child,' she said philosophically, 'it is folly to look and plan too far ahead. Our Greek forefathers said often enough that we are in the hands of the gods. And so, in Christian terms, we are today.'

That night Irene had the strangest dream. She was miles away at the Nicosia airport waiting in the early dawn for the plane from England to arrive. Along it came, down, down, to rest on the tarmac and disembark three passengers – Uncle Herbert, Aunt Ethel and Guy.

They came towards her, and Guy said: 'I've chartered this plane to take you home. Not Josie, though, nor that dog of hers.'

As he spoke he wasn't Guy, any more; he was David exclaiming irritably: 'Come home at once, Irene. The public rooms are a disgrace! No writing-paper, no flowers—'

'Bone lazy. I always said so!' Aunt Ethel's voice. And with that Irene woke up, with the morning sun shining on her face, and the scent of lemon blossom drifting through the window.

CHAPTER FIVE

THERE were no fewer than three last-minute postponements of the trip to Bella Pais.

Some further modernization of the hotel had been planned, and the builders found themselves able to carry out the work sooner than expected. Such an opportunity couldn't be lost in this land where even 'firm dates' could wobble, and everyone engaged in the hotel found themselves caught up in extra work.

Mrs. Vassilou had, with Irene's help, to superintend the moving of all the permanent residents to the top floor, while their usual quarters were brought up to date with private bathrooms. Some of them were far from pleased, not only because of the inconvenience in which they were involved, but because it was clear that they would have to pay more for their accommodation.

Colonel Bykers was, not unexpectedly, the first to complain, and then, shyly and nervously, came along the two English spinsters, Miss Field and Miss Richardson. All had the same lament – their small, fixed incomes simply wouldn't stretch to cover any considerable extra charge.

In the little room behind the office, where Irene had

first been initiated into the workings of the hotel, the very same quartet gathered for tea a few days after the workmen had started operations – Mrs. Vassilou and Irene on one side of the small table, David and Delphine on the other. She and Delphine, she felt certain, were only there as a matter of politeness. Mrs. Vassilou and David were the protagonists. And so it proved.

The old lady was all for 'tempering the wind to the shorn lamb'. It would be absolutely necessary, of course, to raise the terms a little, and she had worked out some figures which she thought, in all the circumstances, fair and proper. The sums she mentioned, looking up from a paper on which she had previously scribbled a few figures, were so modest that even Irene was startled.

As for David, he gave a great sigh of exasperation, and exclaimed: 'Kyria Vassilou, do you want to go bankrupt?'

'If you superintend the work as much as you tactfully can – and watch the costs – we can afford to be generous,' was Mrs. Vassilou's reply. 'These people are here for their health. They are old and find the climate miraculously helpful for the terribly painful arthritis that most of them would otherwise be suffering from.'

'They won't appreciate your generosity, Kyria. That Colonel Bykers, for instance, he's always grumbling.' It was Delphine who spoke.

'You exaggerate, I think. Anyway, he is very kind to that delicate wife of his. His aggressive manner means nothing. And after all, he fought for the Greeks in the last war.'

Delphine shrugged her shoulders: her smile, Irene thought, with a quick spurt of anger, neared the supercilious. But if Mrs. Vassilou noticed that, she gave no sign.

'And now, Irene, your views, please,' she commanded.

'I'm with you, Granny. After all, these people bring us a regular income, which might be a great help in a poor season.'

96

'We're aiming at making the Hermes so comfortable that we shall never have poor seasons,' David pointed out. 'Really, Kyria, you're too quixotic. What about you yourself, when you are old, and need money to live in comfort, after all your hard work?'

Mrs. Vassilou shook her head.

'I've another quotation for you, my children. "Cast your bread upon the waters, and it will return to you again." These people have been here for years. I'm not turning them out. And now that our little conference is over—'

Delphine's smile was openly scornful now, but David's grin held no mockery, only a kind of helpless amusement. This time Mrs. Vassilou did not miss Delphine's contemptuous look.

'I shall make out the bills myself for the next week or two,' she said smoothly. 'I want no more mistakes – or shall we call them misunderstandings – emanating from the office.'

With that she rose to her feet and made her regal exit, and Delphine turned on Irene in a fury.

'She's treated me like this ever since you came!' she exclaimed. 'Wants to push me into giving notice. So I would, this very minute, if I didn't have a child to support.'

'Stop it, Delphine.' David's tone was amiable but decisive. 'Listen! I have to go into Kyrenia on business right away. Bring your shorthand notebook and come along. At once, please.'

'That's just an excuse to get me away, so that I don't present Irene with a few home truths.'

He ignored that remark. 'I did say "at once". That means five minutes. Off with you, now.'

She walked off, and David turned to Irene.

'Try to be patient with her,' he said. 'She's a bundle of nerves.'

'I know. I suppose that's what makes her behave so foolishly – not to me – that doesn't really matter – but to my grandmother. If I'd treated my London employers with such barely veiled insolence, I'd have been out on my ear.'

'I've no doubt of it. But in this little island we're a closely integrated society, cousins umpteen times removed, as often as not. And there's the personal touch. Kyria Vassilou would think of young Theo's welfare before she sacked Delphine.'

'Goodness knows I don't want her to lose her job,' Irene said sharply.

'Don't worry about that. I'll talk sense to her, when we're out. Give her a chance of seeing her kid, too. That should buck her up.' And then he added something that Irene did not find at all palatable. 'She's very loyal to me, I must say that. Backed me up strongly over the necessity of making an extra charge for those modernized rooms. Your grandmother's generosity borders on the crazy, at times.'

'She may have a deeper wisdom than you, David.' Irene had stiffened. 'Anyway, my loyalty is first and foremost to her. Call me a yes-woman if you like!'

She did not catch what he said in reply. She had heard Delphine returning and, preferring to avoid her, disappeared into the office.

She felt distinctly irritated with David. Why did he have to bring loyalty into it? It was true that she had as yet very little knowledge of the financial position of the Hermes. But her grandmother had been running the hotel successfully years before David had come on the scene – though on more modest and old-fashioned lines. She had every reason for faith in her – shared, too, her sympathy for those elderly retired people who could not, try as they might, stretch their fixed incomes to cover higher prices.

Tired and cross, she was cheered more than she might otherwise have been when Andreas rang her up late that evening to confirm the date on which the new club in Nicosia would be opening and to make sure of a definite acceptance of his invitation.

'I must consult my grandmother. But you're absolutely

sure that we shan't be two on our own, Andreas?'

He laughed mischievously. 'Wouldn't it be fine if we were? I'd love that. However, in this archaic little island, where girls have to consult their grandmothers before accepting invitations from their admirers – I can only reply: "painfully sure".'

'I can tell her that your sister and her husband will definitely be there? And some other friends will be in the party, too?'

'Certainly.'

'Very well, I'll go and ask her. And I'll ring you back in about ten minutes.'

As she hung up the receiver and went back to join her grandmother in her sitting-room, she reflected with dry amusement that life was indeed different here than in London. Aunt Ethel had had one great virtue – from the eyes of a young girl – she was not in the least interested in her doings, provided she came in quietly, and was careful not to leave any lights on. She preferred, indeed, to have the family sitting-room to herself – hardly counting Uncle Herbert smoking in his corner – so that she could spread herself and concentrate on the competitions which were to bring her such desirable prizes, in the way of household equipment, cars and the like – if only she persevered.

Mrs. Vassilou listened to her thoughtfully, then asked her: 'What about transport? I couldn't have my granddaughter driving alone in a car late at night – or at any time, come to that – with a young man. These Cypriot men are hot-blooded – your attractive friend, Andreas Nikolaides, being, I am sure, no exception.'

'He's been away from Cyprus long enough for his blood to have cooled down,' Irene observed, smiling. 'Still, I'd much prefer to have someone else around. And I'll tell him it's a definite condition.'

She went back to the telephone to obtain Andreas's assurance on this point – which he gave with a joke or two thrown in – and once again rejoined her grandmother, a smile playing round her lips.

To her surprise, she found David there, drinking a glass of Commanderie which he had just poured out at her grandmother's invitation, and to her annoyance, she found herself flushing.

'Well, my dear, you've arranged matters with the young man?' Mrs. Vassilou handed her a glass of what had come to be her favourite wine.

Aware of David's sharp look, Irene said as airily as she could: 'Yes, everything's settled. The Club opens on Saturday fortnight, and Andreas and his sister and brother-in-law will be fetching me at eight o'clock.'

'Your friend Andreas has pipped me at the post!' David, Irene thought, was also finding it difficult to speak as casually as he would have wished. 'I was going to ask you to come with me – that is, if Kyria Vassilou could spare us both on a Saturday.'

'Of course I could spare you. It's good for the place that I should go over and take charge sometimes.' She looked at Irene. 'I suppose you're too closely committed to this young man to throw him over and go with David instead?'

'Of course she is,' David said quickly. 'In any case, Nikolaides is doubtless a far better dancer than I am.'

'My dear David, don't be so ultra-sensitive. That slight limp doesn't interfere with your dancing at all.' She turned to Irene. 'He's one of the best dancers on the island. Won a cup only last year, down in Limassol.'

He held up his glass to the light before speaking again, as though more interested in the tawny wine than in the conversation.

'A particularly good vintage, this,' he observed. Then, setting it down, he said serenely: 'Dancing apart, Irene must be glad of some fresh company. I imagine he's a gay, amusing sort of chap, this Nikolaides. A real ladies' man.'

It was on the tip of Irene's tongue to say frankly that, as it happened, she would have preferred David as an escort. That if he had shown half the other man's eagerness to secure her as a partner, she would probably be going in his party. But she kept back the words.

David was altogether too self-assured – too casual. The opening of the new club was one of the big events of the year. He had delayed his invitation on the bland assumption that no one else would invite her. It would do him good to be proved wrong.

Another thought occurred to her then. He might very well rejoice at being relieved of a tiresome social duty. He would be free now to transfer his invitation to Delphine, without the Kyria accusing him of slighting her granddaughter.

Instead she said pleasantly: 'But Josie and I have accepted another invitation of yours, don't forget. You're taking us to Bella Pais, in the near future – or so we're hoping.'

'I hadn't forgotten. I'll take you tomorrow – if you're sure you won't be bored.'

She felt like saying: 'Don't be so childish – a great man like you!' But again she thought better of it.

'I'm certain we won't,' she told him amiably. 'Just tell us the time you want to start, and we'll be outside the main entrance waiting – picnic basket, puppy and all.'

Always in after-years she was to remember that expedition to the ruins of that glorious old Gothic Abbey, and to the village which bore its name.

Prince, the puppy, David ruled, must after all stay at home. He would be too restless a passenger for a switchback drive of such length. But before Josie could utter a syllable of disappointment, he told her cheerfully that instead, Theo was to come. He had fixed things with Mrs. Cipriani. They were to pick the boy up at his school as soon as afternoon lessons were over, and return him to his grandmother's house in the early evening.

So to Kyrenia they went, David, Irene and Josie, along the sunny coast road, and found Theo waiting eagerly just inside the school grounds. In a moment he was in the back seat, chattering excitedly to Josie, and off they started, going eastward again, en route for Bella Pais,

101

through the jagged mountains.

As a child Irene had been taken by her parents to visit the old monastery, and had been a little overawed by its great size, its silence, its stately beauty – just as Josie and Theo were to be today.

Now, at twenty-one, those high, gold-tinted ruins, perched on the edge of a fifty-foot cliff, made a different impression on her. The original fourteenth-century building had been called the Abbey of Peace – removed as it was from the haunts of men. And it was not only awe, but a deep feeling of peace that stole upon her now, as the four of them wandered into the grounds where tall, brilliant snapdragons rioted, and magnificent roses, and through cloisters silent except for the chattering of swifts and swallows. Soon they were passing into the vast refectory, still with the birds darting overhead, looking up at the pulpit from which in those long-ago days a monk would read from the Bible to his brethren as they sat at their frugal meals; looking, too, from the traceried windows to the plain below.

Peace! She murmured the word to David, and instead of a mere, responsive smile, his face lit up in a way she had never seen before.

'I love this place more than any other on earth,' he said very quietly. 'And, as you know, I've been about the world a lot. Usually I come here alone, and always I leave it with the feeling of shedding every trouble and care – of a blessing resting on me.' She nodded, and he went on quickly: 'I'm glad you feel it too. If one comes with the wrong person, everything is a little spoiled.'

She glowed inwardly, not because he was paying her a polite compliment, but because, for a moment, at least, she had the experience of being wholly in tune with another human being. An experience so rare as to be precious – memorable.

Although so much of the old building had fallen into ruin, the church still stood and they passed through the great doors into the dim interior, brightened they saw, as their eyes became accustomed to the lack of light, by icons of old familiar saints – St. George and his dragon, St. John the Baptist in his camel-hair garment – and many others.

A young priest was working there, robed in black, his brown hair arranged in a neat bun, Orthodox fashion. He and two boys were making preparations for the service to be held next morning: a friendly trio, surprised and delighted to have visitors, apparently British, who could speak fluent Greek, instead of the usual tongue-tied tourists.

'But of course we speak Greek. We live here. And our mothers are Greek Cypriots.' Josie assumed her most important manner. 'Though my sister and I – well, *our* mother died in a plane crash,' she added soberly.

'God rest her soul!' He crossed himself, then looked down at Theo. 'As for this boy,' he observed, smiling, 'I would guess him to be Cypriot all through.'

'And so I am,' Theo told him very seriously. 'My father died soon after I was born – over in Greece. But my mother does not talk about him. It makes her too sad.' He paused. 'I understand. But I would like so much to know more of him.'

'One day, when her heart has healed, she will talk to you.' The priest laid a kindly hand on the boy's dark, curly head. 'Meanwhile you are, I am sure, her great consolation.'

But now the boy shrugged his shoulders. 'Perhaps,' he murmured indifferently, and bowed politely to receive the young priest's blessing, bestowed on all four of them.

Out in the grounds again, they lingered for a while, even the children spellbound by the stupendous views of the surrounding mountains and valleys, the blue sea, far below, and over the water, in the distance, the lavender coast of Turkey, backed by the snow-capped Taurus Range.

'We must move on now, and climb up to the village,' David decreed after a while. 'Everyone will be shocked, if we get home this evening without visiting it – and sitting under the Tree of Idleness.'

Irene was loath to leave this place, so heart-shakingly beautiful with its noble ruins, its flower fragrance, its atmosphere of long abiding peace. She must come again, as soon as the chance arose, but, as David had laid down, in the right company. To visit the ancient shrine with someone who did not share the sense of its benison, its compelling graciousness, would be a misery.

Theo knowing the way, the children ran ahead, and by the time their elders had caught up with them were sitting triumphantly in the main square under the spreading branches of the famous tree which legend said robbed those who lingered in its shade of all desire, and even of capacity, for work. Neither David nor Irene were in the mood for talking, but after the friendly proprietor had brought them some refreshments – coffee for the grown-ups and soft drinks for the children – they found conversation easier.

There were a few villagers sitting in the square, enjoying a leisurely drink after their day's work, and once they found that their visitors could speak Greek without the least difficulty, they welcomed them with open arms, asking innumerable questions under the supposition, to start with, that David and Irene were husband and wife, who must have married extremely early to have such big children.

'Then you are still only affianced,' was the conclusion drawn from the discovery of their mistake.

'My sister does not mean to marry anybody,' Josie proclaimed, before either David or Irene could explain matters.

'Then she is to be a nun, this beautiful young lady?' A fat old man with crisp black curls and a bald pate looked across with a highly disapproving expression.

'Of course not! She is to be my grandmother's assistant at the Hermes Hotel, one day.'

'And by that time she will have found a good husband. Mark my words, little one.'

'Perhaps finding one for you, too, my child,' came another genial voice.

With a sudden change of mood, Josie looked across at David and chuckled.

'Will you wait for me, Uncle David – say, six years?'

'Then if Miss Irene still doesn't want to marry, she could live with you both,' Theo piped up. 'I might come, too – as head waiter or something, if Mother didn't mind.'

'It sounds a very complicated situation,' was Irene's dry comment.

David drained his coffee-cup.

'Capable of simplification – possibly!' Bored, it seemed, with the conversation, he was concentrating on settling the bill. 'And now we must get moving again if we're to explore the village. Save our breath, too. It's the devil of a climb.'

Some of the villagers pricked up their ears at that.

'It's sitting under the Tree of Idleness makes you feel that way,' was their hilarious verdict. 'If you stay much longer, you'll not get up our gentle slope at all.'

The stony path was steep indeed, and Irene found herself wondering how the older villagers, especially those who lived at the top, could possibly negotiate it. A little breathless herself, she was, however, entranced by the ancient doorways through which one caught a glimpse of primitive cottages with their little gardens, from which children ran with welcoming cries. Their elders, too, were friendly, waving and smiling – and coming down to talk when they found that their visitors spoke Greek.

Quiet as it was, this village in the shadow of its ancient abbey, there were the unmistakable signs of a busy life. A carpenter sawed wood in his small shop, in another a cobbler was working, and the tangy smell of cooking drifted out from kitchen after kitchen.

'Time for our picnic, and then home,' was David's immediate reaction, and soon they were on the homeward journey, eating and drinking in the car instead of finding a place on a hillside, for it was getting late, and soon darkness would be falling.

'If you hadn't waited until after school, you could have

started earlier,' Theo pointed out, as he munched a luscious meat-filled pasty. 'But Mama said I mustn't miss my lessons.'

'Quite right, too!' David told him.

'And that's why I can't stay the night at the Hermes,' Theo continued. 'Lessons. Mama says I must work hard to catch up after going to Miss Taylor's class. But my form-master says something about my not having lost ground at all, that she must be a very good teacher. She's coming to live at Kyrenia, so perhaps—'

'You mean she's leaving the Hermes?' Irene was astonished. She looked across at David questioningly.

He was faintly embarrassed. 'It's all connected with these alterations,' he said. 'Someone – I don't know who – said something very tactless in her hearing, about people who pay a pittance expecting millionaire accommodation. She took it as referring to herself. Her rooms are included in the modernization. I'm sure Kyria Vassilou will persuade her to take no notice. They're such friends. But that little Miss Taylor's intensely proud.'

'If she does move, Josie, you'll be coming into Kyrenia every day.' Theo was already weighing things up, with a wisdom beyond his years. 'But unless she gets a house near our school, or near Granny's flat, we shan't see each other. Anyway, we can have much more fun up at the Hermes than we could down in Kyrenia. Granny has almost no garden.'

'I do wish your mother—' Josie began petulantly; but a look from Irene silenced her, and nothing more was said just then on the subject.

When, after dropping Theo at his grandmother's little flat, the rest of the party went back to Mrs. Vassilou's quarters, they sensed at once that something was wrong. And after Josie, kissed affectionately by her grandmother, had gone up to bed, David and Irene learned why the old lady was looking so disturbed, so angry.

Her guests, she told them stormily, among them some whose friendship she most valued, were being insulted by people who should know better. She hadn't got to the bottom of it yet. But when she did, she was going to show in no uncertain manner who was the owner and mistress of the Hermes.

Not another word would she vouchsafe on the thorny topic. Nor for once did she exercise her customary hospitality by bringing out a comfortably rotund bottle of Commanderie and offering them a nightcap.

'You'll be tired after your expedition,' she told Irene. 'And I'm dropping with weariness myself. Bed is the answer.' And to David she observed briefly: 'We must have a serious discussion tomorrow morning. I'm deeply concerned – and let me say, once and for all, that I expect your close co-operation.'

To that interview next morning came Nicos, Anastasia, the head chambermaid, and Delphine, the two servants looking anxious and mystified, Delphine bored.

Irene was relieved when her grandmother requested her to employ herself as best she could over at the hotel, making up for the absence of these three important members of the staff. After those golden hours of peace at Bella Pais, the idea of plunging into conflict was most repugnant.

Delphine had already begun work in the office: there was nothing urgent, Irene found, to be done there. So she set about doing what she liked best, making the public rooms look as neat and attractive as possible, and chatting amicably to any of the guests who happened along.

She saw nothing of Miss Taylor and learned from Panos that having no class today, she had gone down to Kyrenia on business.

'Do you know what's wrong, Miss Irene?' he asked her. 'The last time there was this sort of summons from the Kyria, Nicos and Anastasia say, it was because a guest lost her handbag and declared that it must have been stolen. She found it, the silly woman, but not before she had threatened to tell the police. They don't want anything like that happening again, they say.' And he added confidently: 'We have faults, we Greeks. But we are proud of our honesty, at least.'

'And with reason,' Irene assured him. 'But just get on with your work, and don't worry. Nicos is pleased with you, he says – so keep it up!'

She was upstairs going round the bedrooms when Anastasia returned to say that the Kyria had given them one of her periodical lectures on the importance of treating every guest with the courtesy and kindness 'worthy of our reputation as Cypriots'.

'She knows that Nicos and I can be relied upon,' she continued, 'but we must not let up, she insists, on our training of our subordinates. She said little to Mrs. Cipriani until she started complaining about young Panos. That upset Nicos, of course, but the Kyria would not let him stay to argue the matter. He could be sure of her justice – and common sense – she said. And so we can. Of Kyrie David's, too. So we came away, Nicos and I, to get on with our work, leaving Mrs. Cipriani to spin a rope of stupid lies long enough to hang herself.'

Later that morning Irene found herself wondering whether this had indeed happened. The first thing that occurred was the arrival of Delphine who, after a few moments in the office, went up, stony-faced, to her bedroom, from which she emerged half an hour later in outdoor clothes. Ignoring everyone in the foyer, she ordered Hercules, the hall-porter, sharply to bring down her luggage and again without a word to anyone walked out into the courtyard. Within moments David had driven up in his car, helped Hercules stow her cases into the boot, and was whisking her away.

Anxious to avoid any attempts to draw her into a discussion of all this, Irene went over now to her bedroom to tidy up before lunch and ran into Josie, playing with her boisterously lively puppy.

'I've been out here all morning,' the little girl told her. 'Granny had what she calls a staff meeting in her room.'

'How grand that you have Prince to play with, darling!'

'I know. But I still miss Theo. We have such fun together, imagining things, and if he could bring his puppy up here, too, it would be absolutely super. *Why* doesn't Mrs. Cipriani like him playing with me?'

'Maybe because she doesn't like me very much.' Irene decided to be frank.

'That's what Theo says. Anyway, we've both got our dogs – and I've got you, and Granny and Uncle David as well.'

It was evening before Irene learned what had passed that morning during the interview with Delphine. And it was her grandmother's version, not David's, that she heard.

Delphine had stoutly denied being intentionally rude to Miss Taylor at any time. Some of the permanent residents were very exacting, requiring far more attention than the ordinary guests, and she might have made an impatient remark to one or other of the staff, having no idea that she might be overheard. It was far more likely that young Panos had been the offender. She had had to speak to him more than once about his manners.

'I pointed out that Miss Taylor would hardly have mistaken a man's voice for a girl's,' Mrs. Vassilou said, 'and she tried then to put the blame on one of the chambermaids. But although Miss Taylor has refused to accuse any particular woman, I am certain in my own mind that Delphine is the offender.'

'Have you sacked her?' Irene asked, worried. She felt strongly that the Hermes would do better without Delphine, but was concerned at the thought of her being out of work, with Theo to keep.

'I would have done, but for David's pressure on me to be lenient. He emphasized that Miss Taylor had not made any accusation against Delphine, also that the girl – if you can call a woman of thirty-odd a girl – was in poor health. Thoroughly overtired and nervy. So I compromised by sending her off on leave at once for a couple of months, giving her – on the strict condition that she consulted the best doctor in Kyrenia – her full salary, plus an allowance for board, and for medical fees.'

Irene's kind heart lightened. 'Then she has no real grievance!'

'She certainly thinks she has.'

'Does David agree with her?' Irene could not repress the question.

'Not really! How could he? It's that sentimental Scottish side of his character. You'd think he was as hard as nails, but when it comes to a damsel in distress – in this case, a young woman with a child to support – he's as soft as putty. Especially,' the old lady added shrewdly, 'if he finds her attractive.'

'Does this mean that Miss Taylor will be staying on?'

'Unfortunately, no! She has decided she wants her own little house. She's very grateful to me, she says, and will be coming up often for a game of cards, when I'm at leisure.'

'But, Granny, will she find anything she can afford?' Irene demanded dubiously.

A faint smile lightened Mrs. Vassilou's classic features.

'I think so. I own some property in the neighbourhood – including a charming little cottage, just becoming vacant, on the outskirts of Kyrenia. It's in the grounds of a bigger house, so shouldn't be too isolated for her. But the affair will have to be handled with the greatest possible tact. So, my dear, not a word to anyone.'

One result of Delphine's suspension was that Mrs. Vassilou took a stronger hold of the reins, and spent far more time at the hotel. Working with her, and watching her, Irene came to understand the reason for the high reputation held by the best type of Cypriot as hotel-keeper and restaurateur all the world over. In the effort to satisfy the reasonable requirements of each individual guest, no trouble must be spared. Even unlikely needs must, if possible, be met. The old laws of hospitality which still prevailed throughout the East demanded this.

But the old lady was not only a philosopher; she had a sound practical knowledge of the workings of the hotel, and paid keen attention to detail. Although, working hard herself, she expected her staff to do the same, they all rejoiced at having her among them again, day in, day out. If she found fault – well, she was equally quick with praise; generous, too, with a warm interest in them and their families.

With so much on hand Irene began to wonder whether she ought to have accepted Andreas' invitation to the opening night of that new and glamorous club at Kyrenia. But when she broached the subject to her grandmother she was told not to be foolish. She had had very little fun since coming to Cyprus. It was high time she had a fling.

'I've been very happy here,' Irene said.

'No regrets for coming?'

'Not one!'

Mrs. Vassilou hesitated a moment, then asked quietly: 'Are you getting over that – that friend in England? Guy, I imagine, his name is, from that fuss Josie made over what her puppy was *not* to be called.'

Irene coloured faintly.

'Yes; he's Guy Cosway. And although I still think about him more than is sensible, memories don't hurt the way they did. It's coming right away that has helped me. If I were still in London, working in the City and running the risk of a sudden meeting, it would be very painful.'

Her grandmother nodded. 'Maybe you'll tell me some time just what went wrong. But I don't want to press you.'

'It was because of Josie – but she must never, never know. I thought I'd never met anyone so kind and sweet-natured, and when he asked me to marry him I took it for granted that Josie would live with us. He knew, so I thought, how much she depended on me, clung to me. But he wouldn't hear of it. To start our life together saddled with a child of nine – those were his exact words – would be sheer madness. He had never heard such a

III

crazy idea.'

'Is he a very poor man?' the old lady asked her.

'Far from it. He has a partnership in his father's very flourishing firm. Oh, he offered to take on quite a lot of financial responsibility for Josie, pay for her to go to a good boarding-school, arrange fine holidays for her – and let her come to us for an occasional week-end. But to live with us – no! And if there's one thing Josie needs, with that tragedy of our parents' death, it's to be cherished in the security of a loving home.'

'Perhaps he'll change his mind. Sorry and distressed as I should be to lose my darling granddaughters, my first wish would always be for your happiness.'

There was such weariness, such sadness, in Mrs. Vassilou's expression that Irene wished she had not succumbed to the temptation of talking about this sorrowful little history.

'Granny dear, although I'm foolish enough to grieve sometimes, when I remember how sweet and loving he could be, how – it used to seem to me – understanding, I've felt more and more strongly since I came here that I could never go back to him, even if he were to offer Josie a home after all.'

'Perhaps you will find a husband here.' Mrs. Vassilou was looking happier. 'Then we could share our precious little Josie, you and I!'

'We can do that anyway, Granny dear, without my marrying anybody! So far as I'm concerned, I'm happy with things as they are. We're devoted to you, Josie and I, and to live here with you in the sunshine—'

'That won't satisfy you for ever, darling. Nature has a way of taking a hand. I did hope—' she hesitated a little – 'that when you came here, David and you—! But Delphine, with her appeal to his sympathy, and kindness of heart, has too firm a hold on him, I'm afraid.'

'I daresay they'd be very happy together,' Irene returned coolly.

'Well, she is not going to queen it at the Hermes in my lifetime,' the old lady said, almost fiercely. 'In fact I should arrange it in my will that she was excluded from any hand in management – if I could. She would ruin all that your dear grandfather and I built up over the years.' And then, her mood changing, she smiled across at her granddaughter. 'You've met very few marriageable men since you came here – but you haven't been here very long. You're an attractive girl, and would have a fine dowry in the shape of a partnership in the Hermes.'

Irene tried to protest that she didn't expect such generosity – couldn't indeed accept it. But her grandmother waved the interruption aside.

'You have plenty of time, and you'll find you have plenty of choice,' she told her. 'And now you must have a new and becoming dress for this function in Nicosia. We'll go to town one afternoon this week and choose something worthy of your looks – and your status in the island.'

That visit to Bella Pais had seemed, at the time, to bring about a better understanding between Irene and David – Irene, at all events, felt that way. But it didn't last.

David showed himself cooler and more reserved than ever. With Mrs. Vassilou back at the helm, there was less reason for him to be in contact with Irene, but he appeared to be deliberately avoiding her.

'It's because he thinks Delphine has been unfairly treated,' she told herself impatiently. 'Not that I care if he chooses to be so damn silly!'

Encouraged by Mrs. Vassilou's interest, and by Josie's excited chatter about 'the Ball', she threw herself, after working hours, into preparations for the great event.

The shopping which preceded it was on a far more lavish scale than she had ever experienced. Leaving David in charge of the hotel, Mrs. Vassilou took her grandchildren into Nicosia by hired car, declaring that it was by far the most comfortable arrangement. A paid chauffeur wouldn't mind how long he was kept hanging about. It would all mean extra money for him. And there was to be no hurry-scurry over choosing the dress and its accessories.

They drove straight to the most exclusive dress salon in the town, where the elegant, firmly corseted proprietress was an old friend of the Vassilous. Her collection, though not large, was superb, and the choice by general consent – Josie, too, allowed a vote! – finally rested between two dresses, both deceptively simple in cut. One was a clinging affair of hyacinth-blue and silver, the other of rose-red chiffon, full-skirted.

The discussion was characteristic of the Middle East. Members of the staff were summoned to give their views, and even one or two customers who happened to be on the premises – acquaintances of the Vassilou family – were invited to join in. Finally, because she was a little tired of choosing blue to match her eyes – and didn't want Andreas renewing his foolish compliments on that score – she decided on the rose-red chiffon. And then came the pleasant task of choosing accessories and the triumphal drive home.

The opening of the Club was to take place on a Saturday, and on the Friday Andreas rang her up to know the colour of her dress. He wanted to send her appropriate flowers, and to confirm that he would be calling for her, in company with his sister and her husband – there was the hint of laughter in his voice at this mention of chaperonage – at eight o'clock on the following evening.

In the event it was freesias he sent – so fragrant that, dressing, they scented the bedroom – and, indeed, the surrounding rooms.

Not one word had David said to her on the subject of the ball, but while she was sitting with her grandmother and Josie, waiting for Andreas to arrive, the old lady observed discontentedly that David was a funny fellow.

Both girls looked up in surprise, and Mrs. Vassilou went on quickly: 'He told me just now that he may be going to the dance himself. Very late, when all the work's done. I told him I could have managed very well without him, and that *he* could have escorted you instead of Mr. Nikolaides. But he said that he, and the party he was possibly joining, would be putting in an appearance very late. Why must he be so secretive? Why couldn't he have mentioned it before?'

'Perhaps he couldn't get a partner,' Josie suggested sympathetically. 'Though I can't see why. If I was big enough to go to the ball, I'd rather have him than anyone. He can look cross sometimes, but he's a very special person, *I* think.'

Before any comment could be made on this, there was the sound of a big car arriving, and in came Andreas and his relations — as if to testify that they were really there. His sister, Maria, was a pretty little girl, very like her brother in looks: her husband, a typically good-looking Cypriot, a good deal older than herself and very much in love with her, it seemed.

They stayed for a little time, chatting — Maria making quite a fuss of Josie, and telling her that she had a dear little girl of two with the very same Christian name. And then off they went, Irene in front with the beaming Andreas, and the married couple behind.

The Club, though spacious in the manner of the Middle East, and decorated in classical style, managed, all the same, to convey a sense of intimacy. It was the lighting and the profusion of flowers, Irene thought, that was responsible, and subconsciously she began to pick up ideas for making the restaurant of the Hermes more attractive.

The friends of whom Andreas has spoken were, it seemed, unable to come: they had left a message of regret with the doorman that they had had a call to a sick relative. Maria and her husband, Michaelis, proved, however, excellent company, and Irene found herself, before long, thoroughly enjoying the evening.

Both Andreas and Michaelis were excellent dancers, with perfect manners, and she quickly shed those small, secret qualms she had entertained about her host's behaviour. The small band, too, was first-class.

Andreas, all set to please her, was intelligent enough to know that any display of over-familiarity would annoy her. Among all these fashionable people dancing here, or sitting at little tables, there must be several who knew Irene by sight, as Kyria Vassilou's granddaughter, and many others who would pick her out as one of the most beautiful and well-dressed young women present.

Relaxed, and thoroughly enjoying herself, she suddenly realized that tonight, for the first time, she could go out dancing, in a strikingly lovely dress, without a painful feeling of regret that it was not Guy who was with her. Although, back in England, she had gone dancing in her teens with a variety of young men, it was only with Guy that she had visited any such glamorous place as this, only with him, indeed, that she had worn formal evening dress – and that, of necessity, something picked up at the Sales.

Tonight, at least, she could feel that she had got over him – to use the prosaic phrase. Though tomorrow might bring back something, at least, of that sense of loss.

Very sensibly, she considered, the management had provided Greek food at its best for supper, together with some of the island's choicest wines – from grapes of a type grown for hundreds of years here in Cyprus, Andreas boasted modestly. And Michaelis went on to speak of a famous two-handed drinking bowl belonging to the sixth century before Christ, found on the site of an ancient town, and bearing, in Greek, the legend: 'Be happy, and drink well!'

It was after supper, and she was dancing with Andreas who, warmed with wine, was holding her just a little more closely than before, that she caught sight of David, looking almost handsome in his evening clothes, coming in with a party. She looked instinctively for Delphine – and saw her at once in a shining gold dress, with golden leaves in her hair.

'Who are you looking at with such interest?' Andreas demanded with a tinge of jealousy. Then, turning to follow the direction in which her glance had gone, he changed colour slightly. And in that split second, Delphine – and not David, as she had expected – met his eyes in a glance of recognition and, more than that, open hostility.

'I didn't realize you and Mrs. Cipriani knew each other so well,' Irene remarked as they returned to their table. 'But of course, you will have met at the Hermes.'

'Of course.' His tone was bland. 'She's quite an important person there, I gather – with matrimonial designs, they say, on her present escort.'

'Andreas, you should not say such spiteful things,' Maria, his sister, exclaimed reproachfully. 'About a pretty girl, too. It's not like you.'

'Oh, I've deteriorated since I went to live abroad,' was his smilingly penitent reply. 'Or maybe it isn't that. Perhaps it's just that we've seen so little of each other for years past, my dear little sister, that you've forgotten my faults.'

Irene, fingering her wine-glass without drinking, was hardly listening to this conversation.

Delphine, as she well knew, had an uncanny gift for making enemies. But why should she look at Andreas with such dislike, such contempt? However rude she might have been to him in recent months, when he had rung up at the office, or called there, there was no need for such animosity. Except that the Greeks had that sharp pride which made them, at times, inclined to quarrel. In any case, she suddenly remembered, Andreas always made a point of ringing her at her grandmother's wing – of calling for her there.

Perhaps there had been a family feud between the Nikolaides and the Ciprianis. For though Delphine's husband had spent most of his life in Greece, so she understood from David, he was a Cypriot by birth. Oh, well, she wasn't really interested. What struck her more insistently was Andreas' remark that Delphine intended to marry David.

It was, as his young sister had pointed out, a spiteful

remark, unworthy of him – wine had doubtless loosened his tongue. But it did show that Mrs. Vassilou's fear of a marriage between David and Delphine was not without foundation.

She would have liked to be able to tell herself that, here again, she had no interest in the matter. But it would not have been true. Once David married Delphine, things at the Hermes would be quite different, whatever efforts her grandmother made to keep the place on an even keel. Delphine was clever and quite unscrupulous, well able to twist the soft-hearted David round her little finger. She simply would not allow herself to be ousted from the Hermes indefinitely. Little by little she would worm her way back.

'And once Granny has gone, there'll be no place for me at the hotel,' Irene reflected. 'Certainly I couldn't work there with Delphine queening it over me, interfering at every turn. Not that I'd be given much chance. She'd soon find a way of getting rid of me.'

Dancing with Michaelis she kept her eyes from straying to the corner where David was sitting with his party. But she was aware, all the same, of the exact moment when David took Delphine in his arms and began to dance with her. Aware, too, during the next few moments, that David, despite his slight limp, was, indeed, a good dancer, as her grandmother had insisted.

She did not expect him to come over and ask her to dance. People, unless on particularly friendly terms, kept to their own parties, on these occasions – so Andreas had told her. And it seemed reasonable. But later something happened to make her wish there was more elasticity in the convention.

While their partners were at the bar, Maria – to her dismay – told her, pleasantly but regretfully, that she and Michaelis would have to leave almost at once, it being such a long drive back to their home. She hoped Irene wouldn't mind. She and her husband had understood that Andreas' friends, who were to have completed the party, would have been accompanying her and Andreas on the drive back to the Hermes. Still, English girls were much freer in this way, she knew. So it couldn't really matter.

'I'm afraid it does!' Irene did not attempt to disguise her annoyance. 'Living with my Cypriot grandmother, I'm expected to behave in the same way as any other Cypriot girl of good family.' And she added quickly: 'Surely if we all leave now, there would be time for you and your husband to see me back to the Hermes first.'

'Out of the question,' was Maria's immediate response. 'We are already late. And the woman we engaged to look after my baby said she could not and would not stay after daybreak. She has her family to care for.'

She signalled to her husband to come quickly, and he left the bar at once, followed at a more leisurely pace by Andreas.

'We must go – and at once, Michaelis!' she exclaimed. 'It is later than I thought. I promised Cassandra that we'd be back before dawn. Oh, how could we have been so careless?'

'Well, off you go! I'll stay behind and settle our bill.' The pair, after the briefest apologies and good-byes, hurried off, and Andreas turned to Irene with the appearance, at least, of concern.

'I'm terribly sorry that this should have happened! Why couldn't those two have watched the time? How could *we* know that their baby-sitter wasn't committed to waiting until their return!'

'In the circumstances you should have surely found that out.' Irene's voice was chilly.

'My dear girl, if those friends of mine hadn't let me down at the last minute—'

She shrugged her shoulders.

'It's very unfortunate. My grandmother will be very displeased!'

'But that's absurd. In England and America – yes, and the Scandinavian countries, too – you would be thought positively eccentric if you objected to a man friend driving you home after a dance.'

Her eyes glinted with annoyance. 'I don't deny it. But we happen to be in Cyprus. And I'm not just an English visitor. I'm making my home with an old-fashioned Cypriot grandmother, who expects and trusts me to respect her conventions.'

'It's time all this narrow-minded nonsense was dropped.' He, too, was looking annoyed now. 'These older people should realize that there's a world beyond this little island.'

'Where the men aren't quite so hot-blooded,' was her thought, remembering the slight difficulty she had had at keeping him at arm's length on that expedition to gather wild flowers on the foothills of the Kyrenia Range. It had been daylight then, and Josie had been within call to play gooseberry if required. A drive by night with Andreas who had dined – *and* wined well – she didn't like the idea at all. Nor would she have done had the scene been transferred to the English countryside, with Andreas still her escort.

'You don't trust me, Irene!' His words startled her by their aptness. But she was certainly not going to admit to any nervousness of him.

'That's not the point,' she said shortly. 'Anyway, it's getting late. We'd better be moving. And please don't think I'm ungrateful to you for giving me such a wonderful time. I've – I've enjoyed myself very much.'

'I'm glad of that, anyway.' His dark, good-looking face cleared. 'I'm sorry for my carelessness – really and truly!'

'I blame myself, too, for not making sure that everything was in order. And I'm sure you'll behave like a gentleman, Andreas, and not start any nonsense.'

He took her arm and pressed it, as they made their way to the foyer, past the table where David and his party were still sitting.

'You can rely on me, my darling, I promise,' he murmured into her ear, and leaving her to pick up her Chinese silk shawl from the cloakroom, he went off to get the car.

And then something happened. Through the swing doors, close behind her, came David, alone and looking grim.

'I've fixed for Delphine to be taken home by friends,' he said curtly. 'I'm taking you back to the Hermes. That Adonis of yours has had as much wine as he can carry – I was watching him while he was at the bar just now. And even if he hadn't—!'

Irene hesitated, utterly relieved, but nervous, too, over how she should behave. If Andreas and David indulged in a row in the foyer of the new club over who was to take her home, her reputation would be in shreds.

'Come,' he said evenly. 'You've only to get into my car, which is parked a few yards away. I'll explain matters to your friend. It only makes sense, my taking you back when our destination is precisely the same.'

She did not pause to consider that in carrying out David's orders – for there was really no other name for them – she would still be driving through the night, alone with a man. But that aspect of the situation did not, it turned out, escape Andreas.

She had been sitting in David's car for no more than three minutes, when along came Andreas, with David close behind.

'Good night, my dear,' he said smoothly. 'Evidently these conventions, so oddly important to an English girl, can be manipulated with delightful ease. Mr. MacLeod thinks you will agree with him that, as your cousin, and fellow resident at the Hermes, it is more fitting that he should see you home. After all, who am I, but your unfortunate host?'

'I'm sorry, Andreas, but it is really a more sensible arrangement.' So glad was she to evade that solitary drive with him, that she could afford to be gracious. 'I'm most grateful, let me say again, for a lovely evening.'

'Good night, Nikolaides.' David was beside her now, letting in the clutch.

But Andreas understandably, so Irene thought with some sympathy, did not think it necessary to return the greeting. He turned and went back, not in the direction of his car, but into the club.

'Perhaps, for all her black looks, Delphine will let him run her home,' Irene thought. 'He's in the mood now to kiss any girl, and if she's annoyed at David's leaving her in the lurch—'

'Aren't you going to show a gleam of gratitude to me for rescuing you?' came David's voice suddenly.

His tone irritated her. 'From a fate worse than death?' she gibed.

He gave her an impatient glance.

'From being pawed about by an amorous chap who gave you his word he'd take you home in a party. Be your age, Irene!'

'He couldn't help his arrangements going wrong. If you'd listen for a minute—'

'I don't want to hear! Whatever his excuses, I'm sure he intended from the first moment of his invitation to you, that things would work out like this.'

'I don't know why you're so down on him,' Irene snapped. 'Maybe because he's one of the many people whom your friend Delphine clearly dislikes!'

'What nonsense. She doesn't even know the man!'

'I don't believe that!'

'And you're the one who accuses me of prejudice.'

'I'm justified. It's impossible to hold a rational conversation with you.'

'Then I suggest we don't try talking to each other.'

'Suits me fine!'

They finished the rest of the short drive to the Hermes in silence. But at the end, as he opened the car door for her, and set her down in her grandmother's little porch, she told him angrily: 'I hope you're pleased at having spoiled my whole evening!'

He looked down at her in the fading glimmer of the stars.

'Deprived you of some passionate embraces?' he mocked, in equally furious tones. 'Here we go then – as a poor substitute!' And sweeping her into his arms he kissed her hard on the lips. Then, releasing her as quickly, he jumped into his car and drove towards the garage by the main building.

CHAPTER SIX

So angry was Irene that she slept little for what remained of the night. How dared David behave in that brutal, oafish fashion – kissing her with a contempt that most men would not show to a woman of the streets?

She could hardly complain to her grandmother. An open rupture between the old lady and this man who had made himself so valuable to her might have disastrous consequences. The odds were that he would walk out in a fury, leaving Mrs. Vassilou to cope as best she could while she looked for another manager, someone equally capable and equally trustworthy in business matters. Someone by no means easy to find.

No, she would have to cope with the situation herself – make David see that she would not stand for such treatment from him. At the very first sign of disrespectful behaviour on his part, she would give him a lashing with her tongue that he would not quickly forget, nor wish to experience again.

Both her grandmother and her little sister commented on her tired looks at breakfast – a meal which the three of them as usual took together – but she made a great effort to assure them that this was only due to dancing so late, and to the pleasurable excitement of the evening.

They were both full of questions – Mrs. Vassilou wanting to know who of her numerous friends and acquaintances were there, and what clothes they were wearing, Josie being chiefly concerned with the supper dishes.

'I'm not interested in other grown-ups' clothes because I'm sure no one looked half as nice as Irene in her lovely red dress,' Josie asserted, digging into her grapefruit. 'And I'm not surprised at her being tired. The flowers she was wearing were as dead as dead this morning.'

'Freesias never last,' Irene returned quickly, smothering the thought that David's roughness, as he held and kissed her, in the early hours, would have finished off any flowers.

And then to her relief her grandmother started off on a completely different topic. Instead of asking awkward questions about Andreas and his relatives bringing her back after the ball, as arranged, she inquired meditatively whether Irene knew how to drive a car.

'A little. But I've never had any lessons, Granny!'

'Except from Guy,' Josie piped up. 'He used to let you try out his Rover last summer,' adding in dismay, flushing: 'Oh, I didn't mean to say that!'

'It's all right, darling.' Irene could see that the child was near tears. 'Granny knows all about Guy.' And to her grandmother she went on: 'I've driven a little, but never in traffic. Guy got me a learner's licence, and I was to have had proper lessons this summer. But – well, I came here instead.'

'Then you might like to have some here,' the old lady said easily. 'It would be a great help to me if you could drive, and would save David time for attending to more urgent matters. He has too much fetching and carrying to do.'

'I'd like to learn. But I'd rather be taught by someone from a Kyrenia garage than by David.' She must, she felt, make that point at once. 'It's a mistake, I think, having lessons from someone you know too well.'

'As you please, my dear. The main thing is that you should become a capable driver without overmuch delay. Then I shall buy you a car of your own.'

'Oh, I shouldn't expect that!' Irene exclaimed.

'And you can, within reason, choose your own model,' Mrs. Vassilou persisted.

'A small second-hand one, suitable for short distances – that's all I should need then. I could shop for you, and take Josie into school. By the way, has Miss Taylor said any more about moving?'

'I'd like you to have a decent car, so you could take Josie and me to visit some of the family. That's my first comment. The second is that, to my great regret, Miss Taylor has already heard of a little bungalow type cottage on the outskirts of Kyrenia and is seriously thinking of renting it. She has been very sweet about it, but apart from anything else, is keen to have a real little school of her own, not just a class, as she has here.'

Josie's eyes sparkled. 'It would be fun to go and see it. And perhaps if it's a real school, Theo will be allowed to come there, too.' She looked at her grandmother. 'Prince is grand, but I do miss Theo, you know. He's so good at make-up games – which are what I like best, too.'

'I doubt if that will be possible, darling. But I'll try to persuade his mother to let him come up more often at week-ends. He would have better food here, and much more fun.'

'Perhaps Uncle David could manage it,' Josie suggested. 'You know, Granny, I think he's one of the few people that Mrs. Cipriani likes. Panos thinks so, too.'

Both Mrs. Vassilou and Irene looked startled at this, and when Josie, having finished breakfast, went off in search of Miss Taylor, the old lady said, frowning a little: 'Josie ought to have more companionship of her own age. There's too much coming and going with the children who are brought by their parents to stay at the Hermes, no time to form friendships. Panos is a good boy, but – well, perhaps Josie is right. I must have a word with David over Theo's coming here more often.'

'Delphine's main complaint is that very difficulty – a difference in age,' Irene pointed out.

'It doesn't count in this particular case,' was Mrs. Vassilou's crisp retort. 'And well she knows it. Or would, if she wasn't so blinded by jealousy.'

A word with David was the last thing Irene wanted, but while she was over in the pantry that morning, arranging fresh flowers for the restaurant, he came in, finding a moment when no one else happened to be in the cool, white-tiled room.

He came up to her quickly, his limp scarcely impeding him at all, and said steadily: 'I've come to apologize. To force kisses on a woman who dislikes one is unforgivable. I give you my word it will never happen again.'

'I should hope not. But my point of view is wider. To show such contempt to a woman you detest as to kiss her in that fashion – almost with hatred—!'

'Irene, that's not true! I resented you at first, certainly. And you still make me furious at times. But if you were to go away, go back to England—'

'There's not much likelihood of that, my dear David! I've burnt my boats.' Her voice was as icy as ever. 'There's only one way for you and me to get on without flying at each other – and that's a policy of avoidance.' She paused for a moment, then went on haughtily: 'My grandmother likes to remind me that you're a distant cousin of mine. I suggest that as far as possible you keep your distance.'

'That's O.K. by me. But did Kyria Vassilou tell you she wants me to give you driving lessons?'

'She didn't get as far as that! The moment she began talking about my learning to drive, I made it clear that I didn't want you as my teacher.'

'You really are a little spitfire, Irene! And how crazy to give you a name that means "peace".'

Before she could find a crushing reply to this, Nicos and another waiter came in to polish up the table silver, and David, with a brief nod to the two men, took his departure.

Not till she heard him drive off in the estate wagon, on his almost daily visit to the market, did she give up putting unnecessary final touches to the flower vases, and go to the office. The mail had arrived, and Mrs. Vassilou was sorting it with quick, capable fingers.

'One for you, my dear –from England.' She passed over an envelope to Irene. 'Go into the inner office and read it in peace, if you like. You don't look yourself at all. Still tired, I expect, after last night's festivities.'

'I'd rather get on with the work, and leave it until

later.' The handwriting on the envelope – Guy's handwriting – had given her such a shock that her voice was trembling.

'As you please, my dear. There's plenty to do, goodness knows. Go upstairs and see if the workmen have finished any of the suites on the second floor. I doubt it, but we must keep them up to the mark.'

Pushing the envelope into the pocket of her overall, Irene went on her way.

Her grandmother, she felt sure, would have seen that the letter came from Guy. He had written the customary few lines at the back of the envelope, indicating the name and address of her correspondent. The old lady could hardly have missed it.

'She knows it's bound to disturb me, one way or another,' she thought. 'Wants to give me the chance to recover myself from the shock of hearing from him.'

And indeed she was right. Mrs. Vassilou, a beautiful and desirable young woman in her day, had received quite a few love-letters and tokens, despite her mother's eagle eyes, before she had decided to marry young Vassilou. She could still remember one or two of the boys for whom she had nourished a *tendresse*. The thrill of passionately adoring notes smuggled in to her by sympathetic servants.

It was foolish, she told herself, to worry over the contents of this young Englishman's letter to her granddaughter. One's fate was in the hands of the Divine Power. If it was for Irene's happiness to return to England, and marry this man, Guy Cosway, so be it. 'Only,' she prayed, 'let me, dear God, keep the little one, at least.'

Leaving the second floor, and the workmen's eloquent explanations for the delay in obtaining various essential materials, Irene came down to the landing where dispossessed residents had been given temporary accommodation. She visited them all in turn – all who were still indoors – chatting sympathetically over their various difficulties, and charming away the occasional grumble.

127

She came finally to Miss Taylor's quarters, where – for there were no classes on this particular Saint's day – Josie was enjoying herself helping the old governess to pack up some of her most precious belongings.

'Have you come to soothe *my* feathers, too?' Miss Taylor asked her with dry humour. 'With so many doors opening and shutting, we couldn't help hearing scraps of conversation. Really, my dear, your tact and patience – and yes, your sweetness – do you great credit. You're an asset to this place already, and will be more and more, as time goes on.'

'I like people. And I'm anxious to keep up my grand-parents' tradition,' was Irene's response. But her thoughts shot back to her recent encounter with David – the epi-thet of 'spitfire' which he had hurled at her. He was one person, at least, who exhausted her patience and good temper.

'Miss Taylor says I can go down with her to Kyrenia this afternoon and see the little house she's found.'

Josie, hopping round happily, was full of the joy of life.

'I've pretty well made up my mind to rent it,' Miss Taylor explained. 'It's in the grounds of a much bigger house, quite near it, so I shouldn't feel too solitary. You don't mind my taking Josie along to see it? I'd invite you, too, but a friend is taking us in her very small car. There just isn't room.'

A few months ago – no, a few weeks, only – Josie would have begun to fret at the idea of leaving Irene behind. Now – and what a good thing it was! – she was beginning to react like any normal child.

'I'll tell you all about it when we come back,' she promised her sister. 'Oh, and Miss Taylor says that when she settles down I shall be able to bring Prince along. And maybe Theo will come with his puppy, if Uncle David will talk nicely to Mrs. Cipriani.'

Secretly, Irene was deeply thankful to have the after-noon to herself. She would skim through her letter, the first minute she had to herself this morning. And then, in the siesta time, she would read and re-read it without interruption; pretend to Josie that she was asleep, if she came to speak to her before setting off with Miss Taylor.

In the event, as so often, she found herself with no free time at all. She had no chance of even a quick look at the letter, until the siesta hour. Then, nervously, she opened it and read it – quickly the first time, then more slowly.

'Irene darling,' he wrote,
'I expect you will have heard by now from your aunt and uncle that they have been in touch with me over a book which I lent you, and which your aunt quite unnecessarily returned.

I made a point of calling on them to thank them – also unnecessarily, I suppose, as I could have written or telephoned. But I was aching for news of you.

Don't you think it was rather cruel of you, Irene, not to leave your Cyprus address with me, after my asking you for it? To shut the door so firmly in my face, after all we had been to each other, all the happy times we had spent together. For you *were* happy with me, Irene. You often said so!

Well, I am eating humble pie now – climbing down from my previous stand.

If you will come back and marry me, I'm willing now to have young Josie with us for her holidays whenever she wants to come.

I can't give way further. I still feel convinced that it would be a great mistake to have her with us all the time. It's not just selfishness and hardness of heart on my part, as you seem to suppose. Most people would agree with me that a young married couple should be left to themselves for the first year or two, at least – even perhaps postponing babies of their own.

Could Josie not continue living with her grandmother, if the idea of a good boarding-school in England doesn't appeal to you? Sometimes she could come to us for holidays – sometimes we could go to Cyprus!

Do think this over, darling. Don't give me an impulsive "No". I still love you – miss you badly.

Guy'

She did, indeed, read and re-read that letter, lying out on the balcony, in her long wicker chair. Ironically, though the time of orange-blossom in the hotel garden was nearly over, the fragrance still lingered – bringing the memory of hopes and dreams which had filled heart and mind only a few months ago.

Presently she heard Josie getting up from her bed, and, pushing the letter under her cushion, she shut her eyes, pretending to be asleep. She didn't want to speak to anyone – certainly not to Josie.

Soon the little girl crept out to look at her, then tip-toed away, to run lightly downstairs and out at the front door. So eager, it seemed, to go on this trip with Miss Taylor that she had cut short her siesta, and would now have to wait about for her.

Now Irene could bring out the letter again.

Guy still loved her. Surely if that were so, everything else would fall into line. And what a consolation it was to know that his feelings had not changed, in view of David's crude, contemptuous treatment of her last night. Guy, darling Guy, was incapable of such behaviour to any woman. He didn't, certainly, see eye to eye with her on everything – but he was a chivalrous gentleman. Even Andreas, for all his charm, couldn't touch him for good manners, good breeding, and as for David—

Soothed, she began for the first time to wonder if there was something after all in Guy's point of view. Would any man of his age want a girl of nine around all the time, just when he was settling into marriage? And might he not be right in suggesting that Josie should continue living here with her grandmother?

Hadn't the old lady made it clear that if she were to lose her elder granddaughter, she would be eager to keep the younger with her? If Josie were loved and wanted, would she not settle down – with the holidays to look forward to three times a year?

Surely, young as she was, the thought of her big sister's happiness would thrill her. She would have the excitement of helping to choose the trousseau, of acting as bridesmaid – 'For of course I should be married from here,' Irene thought. Surely, now, there would be nothing to fear on Josie's account. Indeed, she reflected wryly, she herself might suffer more than Josie from an enforced parting. She had mothered Josie for so long – and if Guy should find that he wanted to postpone the arrival of babies, not just for a year or two, but indefinitely—

Well, she must try to put the whole matter to the back of her mind, at least while she was working, or she would be making countless mistakes. It wasn't as though she had to come to an immediate decision. Guy had asked her to think things over, and this she could only do when she was alone and quiet.

She was over in the office writing out the menus when Josie came running in, looking for her, all excitement over Miss Taylor's 'darling little house'.

'I'd love to hear about it, pet, but I'm busy now. You'll have to wait until supper.'

'Can't I help you?'

'If you're very, very careful. Here's a pen with a nice fine nib. You can copy what I've written on this menu card.'

Propped up with a cushion on one of the office chairs, Josie set to work, and writing very slowly, the tip of her tongue much in evidence, produced excellent results. When the cards were all finished, the pair went along to the restaurant to hand them over to Nicos, who, when Josie handed him some she had done herself, assured her that they should be put on the tables of the most important people.

'So long as you give one to Miss Taylor,' Josie insisted, her eyes sparkling. 'She's always talking to me about taking more trouble. And sure, I've taken enough this time.'

She went skipping round the tables then with Irene,

then into the other public rooms, helping to tidy them unobtrusively – though most of the guests were out on the verandas now, sipping cocktails, or upstairs dressing for dinner.

Mrs. Vassilou found them there, and had, of course, to wait while Josie dashed into the restaurant to borrow one of the menu cards she had written.

'Very good indeed,' was Mrs. Vassilou's comment. 'I see that if Irene were to take wing one day I should still have a granddaughter to help me here.'

'Take wing?' The child looked up at her with a mystified expression. 'Do you mean, fly away somewhere? Irene would never do that!' And she pressed herself against her sister. 'Now we've found you, Granny, and got used to everything, we aren't either of us ever going to leave you – or go away from Cyprus. And Irene and me, we're always going to be together.'

So confident she was of what she was saying that she didn't even look at Irene for reassurance, or she might have seen momentary dismay in her big sister's blue eyes. Nor did Mrs. Vassilou notice. Her whole attention was centred just then on the younger girl.

Later, when the three of them were having supper in Mrs. Vassilou's cosy sitting-room, Josie had the chance of describing the cottage which Miss Taylor had almost decided to rent. It was very pretty and not far from a big house where some important people lived: just a tiny walk away, in fact.

'Like a dolls' house, it is,' Josie declared, as she ate with enjoyment her delicious *koupepia*. 'All painted white, inside and out.'

'Is it really big enough for a school?' Irene asked her doubtfully.

'Quite!' It was Mrs. Vassilou who spoke now. 'I know it well. Apart from the kitchen and bathroom, there are two good-sized rooms and two small. A nice little attic, too.'

'I didn't realize you knew it, Granny,' Josie exclaimed.

But Irene told her, smiling: 'I guess Granny knows most of the houses around these parts.'

Mrs. Vassilou nodded. 'And I happen to own quite a few,' she said, adding complacently: 'My granddaughters will not lack dowries.'

Rather fortunately, Irene felt, Josie was too absorbed in her description of the cottage to digest this last remark.

'There's a lovely little garden all round, with a path leading up to the hillside, with woods where we can go for nature study,' she told her elders. 'And we'll do some of our lessons on the veranda. It's really a fairy-tale place.'

'And when do you expect to go there?' Irene asked her. 'I shall have to get going with my driving lessons, I see.'

'We'll be starting the autumn term there – Miss Taylor hopes. Oh, and what do you think? She may have two children as weekly boarders. They'd sleep in the attic.'

'Is that what you'd like, darling? To stay in the fairy-tale cottage all week, and come to us at week-ends?' Mrs. Vassilou was smiling at her. 'We'd miss you dreadfully, but if it would be more fun for you, with Theo coming here so seldom—!'

'Gracious, no, Granny!' Josie almost dropped her fork. 'It might be fine for some children, but not for me! Even with Miss Taylor, I'd be so homesick without Irene – and without you, too, Granny, of course – I'd just pine away.'

Mrs. Vassilou laughed. 'Like a fairy-tale lady! Now, eat up your supper, darling. Here you are, and here you shall stay.'

It was hardly what Irene wanted to hear just then – the confirmation that Josie was still clinging to her – but she was in sufficient control of herself to appear indulgently amused.

When Josie was upstairs and in bed, however, and she and her grandmother were alone, Mrs. Vassilou, sensing her restlessness, said quietly: 'You mustn't take that child too seriously, you know. She's changing already. When she first came here she would have shied away at the idea of going out for the whole afternoon without you. Today she didn't turn a hair!'

'I know.' Irene twisted her hands in her lap, then asked as casually as she could: 'Did you know, Granny, that I had a letter from Guy Cosway today?'

The old lady nodded.

'I couldn't help seeing the name and address on the envelope flap.' She paused – a question in her dark eyes.

After a brief silence, Irene told her: 'He still wants to marry me – makes the conditions a little easier now.' Then from her handbag she drew the letter and passed it over to her grandmother. 'Read it for yourself, Granny. And take your time. I'm going out for a breather, before I go to bed.'

Every day now the weather was noticeably warmer, and it was a relief to get out into the garden, to breathe the cool night air. The moon rode high in the sky so that it was nearly as light as day, and a tiny breeze brought the heady scent of flowers. But for once the island's beauty made no conscious impact on her. She was thousands of miles away, walking with Guy in a London park, his arm slipped through hers, his head bent towards her as he told her how much he loved her – and always would – how he longed to have her to himself, to show her how much she meant to him.

She closed her eyes and stood still for a moment, as though to savour that magic memory to the very full, and started violently when someone else, also out for a breather, sprang up from nowhere and a man's voice – very different in *timbre* from Guy's – demanded: 'Am I forgiven, Irene?'

'What a fright you gave me, David, stealing up on me like that.' She spoke more sharply than she realized, and he countered at once, coolly now: 'If you hadn't been so rapt in your dreams, you'd have heard me coming. My limp would prevent my creeping up to you without a sound. Even if that happened to be my way of behaving.'

'Well, I don't care to have my dreams invaded,' she snapped.

'My dear, I've no key to your particular dreamland. I can only surmise. Come to that, you've no key to mine, for hulking brute as I am, I also dream.'

'I've never said you were a hulking brute!' Deliberately now she was drawing him away from talk of dreams – it might prove dangerous. 'I think you're difficult – and quarrelsome. And as you consider me a spitfire, it's clear that the less we see of each other, the better.'

'In other words, you aren't prepared to accept my apology, and start fresh?' Then, when she fumbled for a rational and dignified reply, he went on quickly: 'I can assure you that I'll never kiss you again, willing or unwilling, if that's what you're afraid of. I'd as soon kiss a tiger!' And off he went, striding fast, but with that limp of his more noticeable than ever before.

She had no wish to stay any longer in the moonlit garden. He had torn those dreams of Guy to shreds with his blundering nonsense. But somehow she couldn't, at this moment, feel angry with him – she could only laugh. 'I'd as soon kiss a tiger!' She had been called a good many things in her time, mostly complimentary, but, among less pleasing epithets, never one quite so colourful. Even Aunt Ethel lagged far, far behind!

She was still chuckling when she rejoined her grandmother, who looked very surprised indeed at this change of mood.

'What's the joke, darling?' she inquired.

'Oh, I ran into David and he said something that tickled me,' Irene returned laconically. 'A silly kind of thing that doesn't bear repeating. But tell me, Granny, what do you think of Guy's letter?' She sighed, all amusement suddenly gone now. 'Isn't life complicated!'

'I don't find it so, my dear. But then I'm a simple person, when it comes to the emotions. The point is, do you love this man and want to spend the rest of your life with him? If so, go ahead and marry him. Everything else will fall into place once you've made your decision.

Made it either way!'

'But the problem is still there. How can I break it to Josie that we shan't be able to live together? You heard the way she went on this evening, about pining away.'

'A very ridiculous phrase, too. I can't think where she got it from – unless from one of the maids in a lovesick mood.' Then she went on very seriously, speaking as nearly always now in the Greek which came so much more easily to her tongue than English: 'Now, listen, Irene! If this man you call Guy had been one of us, he would probably have looked at things differently; been ready to take Josie on as a member of the household without a second thought. But that's because we're such a closely-knit people, with such a strong sense of family. If we marry someone, we just naturally consider their relatives our own.'

'Plenty of people in England take on children who aren't related to them at all,' Irene argued. 'Look at the number of married couples who adopt homeless babies!'

'Newly-married couples?' Mrs. Vassilou queried shrewdly.

Irene evaded a direct answer.

'Guy has known, since we first met, that I've been mothering this young sister of mine, ever since our parents died in that awful crash. He seemed to understand. But he evidently hasn't an inkling of how Josie clings to me, trusts me.'

'My dear, our little Josie would fret for a while, but she would soon recover. She's grown fond of me, and knows how much I love her. She'd have a happy and settled home with me, please God, until she herself found a good husband.'

'I know you'd look after her. And that makes an enormous difference to me. It's a big concession on Guy's part, too, that I could be with her for all her holidays.'

Mrs. Vassilou hesitated. Then she said gently: 'Don't be hurt, my darling. But in the course of time, having her day-to-day interests here – and her friends – Josie may not always want to come to you. She's only a child, and children have short memories.' Then, seeing Irene's startled expression, she went on quickly: 'You, too, might not feel quite the same. You would be building up a life spent largely without her – a life centred on a young family of your own, please God.'

Irene nodded slowly. 'I suppose you're right. I've been living in the moment, not looking so far ahead. But, Granny, there's not only Josie to be considered. There's you. I knew, in my heart, when I came here that you'd probably be hoping that I'd make a career in the Hermes – keep up the family tradition.'

'That's true.' The old lady paused, before continuing diffidently: 'This man, Guy – would he have any interest in hotel management?'

'I'm afraid not. He's in his father's shipping firm, and doing very well. His feet are firmly in the City of London.'

'A pity. That would have been such a wonderful solution!'

'But, Granny, you couldn't have displaced David!' Irene did not realize how shocked she looked – or the faint surprise this caused her grandmother.

'Oh, he's as independent as they come. I shouldn't be surprised if he turns on me one day for being unfair to this tiresome Delphine – marries the creature, and sets up in a hotel of his own.'

'Would he really do that?' Irene's blue eyes opened wide.

'Nothing that David did could surprise me,' Mrs. Vassilou said shortly. Then she added, a smile returning to her face: 'It looks as though I must be prepared to keep going until Josie grows up and marries someone here – a distant cousin, by choice. Now she's shedding that nervousness, she's showing herself a very bright child indeed – as Miss Taylor agrees. I can see her running the Hermes most efficiently one of these days.'

'Don't plan too far ahead just yet,' Irene said quickly. 'Guy wants me to take time before I give him a definite answer. It's a big decision to make, and I must think hard!'

'Of course, my dear,' was her grandmother's smooth reply – but her eyes as she began to neaten the room, prior to going up to bed, were thoughtful.

The next day gave herself and Irene something else to think about. David's father, Colonel MacLeod, rang up to say that he was anxious to talk to Mrs. Vassilou and David on a business matter, and that his wife would very much like to make the acquaintance of her granddaughters. Would it be convenient if they came over from Limassol on the following Saturday and stayed until Sunday evening – possibly taking the two girls back with them for a little change?

'Of course you must come,' the hospitable Mrs. Vassilou told him at once. 'A glimpse of you and dear Amaranth will give us all the greatest pleasure.'

'I didn't commit you and Josie to staying with them,' she told Irene, when she had given her the news of this visit from David's parents, 'but if you're trying too hard to come to a decision over this young man, Guy, a complete change might help you see things more clearly.'

'But, Granny, with Delphine away, there's too much work to be done,' Irene protested. 'I don't want to sound conceited, but I don't see how I could be spared.'

'My dear, David and I would manage – and we've some well-trained staff, you know.' She smiled, and added: 'They like working for you – and with you, it seems. They speak in most flattering terms of you, and your charm and consideration.'

'I'm glad of that. I like them, too.' Irene had flushed a little with pleasure. 'But more than anything, I think it's my being one of the family that counts.'

David, his manner elaborately polite, though decidedly cool, said nothing to her whatever about his parents' proposed visit beyond what was absolutely necessary. And if he noted that a particularly nice bedroom was allotted to them, with the finest view – and the finest bed-linen, too – he gave no sign.

From the moment Irene met Colonel and Mrs. Mac-Leod she knew that she was going to like them. She had gone over to the office, when Josie came running to summon her to their grandmother's sitting-room.

'Uncle David's parents have arrived,' she cried excitedly. 'They're very nice and they've brought us some lovely presents. We're going to have tea as soon as you come.'

Irene smiled down at her.

'All right, darling, let's go. I must just tell Hercules to keep an eye on things.'

'Oh, you'll have to go alone, I'm afraid. I've got to go and find Uncle David. They're here a bit sooner than they expected.'

And off she went – happy, important and thoroughly at home.

'So this is Irene!' Mrs. MacLeod, small, dark-haired and plump, held out her arms. 'And you've really come to live in your dear mother's homeland? I remember you well as a child, very like Josie is now, but I'd begun to think I should never see you again.'

Then Colonel MacLeod, also kissing her, explained: 'On our occasional trips to Europe we spend all our time in the Highlands of Scotland. Our free time, that is. Visiting vineyards in the wine-growing countries – well, it's enjoyable, but more of a busman's holiday.'

'I hear you're a great help to your grandmother at the hotel,' Mrs. MacLeod went on.

'Indeed she is!' Mrs. Vassilou looked across at Irene affectionately, but with a faint wistfulness which only the girl herself noticed – and interpreted.

'Well, I hope David doesn't bully you,' Mrs. MacLeod went on, smiling broadly. 'My husband's a holy terror, I may tell you.'

'Don't you believe her, Irene. She's half my size, but makes up for it by cunning. Always gets her own way.'

'It's not my cunning that's made you more amenable. It's living in the sun all these years.'

'Then maybe in time our very dear but rather formidable David will mellow,' Mrs. Vassilou observed with dry amusement. 'I think I'm the only person at the Hermes who isn't just a little scared of him.'

'I'm not – and I don't think Irene is, either!' Josie had just returned, a little breathless, to hear the end of the conversation.

'You're two very attractive girls – that alters matters!' Colonel MacLeod slipped his arm round the child. 'But what have you done with him?'

'He's over in his room at the hotel, changing his shirt. He showed it to me. It's a new one.'

'Josie, you shouldn't go trespassing like that, dear!' Irene exclaimed.

'Well, Hercules was busy on the telephone, so I thought I'd nip up. I knew he wouldn't want to miss a minute with you,' and she smiled across at the MacLeods. 'After all, he is our uncle – in a way!'

Panos, proud of his responsibility, came from the kitchen now with the tea tray and set the things out neatly on Mrs. Vassilou's lace-trimmed tablecloth. And shortly afterwards along came David – as Josie had indicated, spruced up for the occasion. Looking at him in company with his father, Irene thought how alike they were. The only way in which he resembled his mother, so far as she could see, was in that sudden smile of his. Both had something of mockery in it, though in her case the humour was far gentler.

It was a cheerful tea-party, with Prince, allowed in for once in a way at a meal, behaving beautifully, lying down under the table, and only whimpering occasionally at the thought of the cake which the humans were enjoying.

Much of the conversation centred on the girls' parents. Their mother had been a great friend of Mrs. MacLeod, as well as a distant relation. They had been at school together, gone to the same dances and other festivities, had attended each other's weddings in Nicosia, each marrying a man from Britain.

'One of these days, when you come to stay with us at Limassol, I'll show you some amusing old photographs,'

Mrs. MacLeod promised. 'I suppose we must wait until you're fairly slack at the hotel, Irene being so valuable now.'

'I hope we shall never be slack at the Hermes now,' David observed nonchalantly. 'We're modernizing fast. But time off is a necessity for everyone. If Irene would like to pay you a visit, we could manage, couldn't we, Kyria?'

'Of course. But transport is the difficulty at the moment. As soon as Irene learns to drive with confidence, and has her own car, she'll be able to manage the journey.'

'We could take them back with us tomorrow,' Mrs. MacLeod remarked briskly. 'But I suppose David would have to fetch them, and that means leaving you alone here, my dear.'

'Then we must postpone it for a while,' Colonel Mac-Leod said placidly. 'Some time before the winter they must come – and then in the spring, without fail. The Limassol Carnival is out of this world.'

'When they get used to the journey I hope they'll come often,' was Mrs. MacLeod's final contribution. And she added, chuckling: 'If David is their uncle, you and I, dear, must be great-aunt and great-uncle. Though I must say, it doesn't feel quite like that.'

And then David took a hand in the conversation.

'I'm certainly Josie's uncle – by courtesy and affection – but hardly Irene's! I've no ambition to establish such a relationship with her.'

It was, although David spoke lightly enough, an awkward moment – for Irene, at least. But she managed to laugh.

'Nor I,' she said. 'He'd boss me more than ever.'

Altogether the MacLeods' visit was a great success. Everyone liked them, and it was not only because of David's position at the Hermes that the staff surpassed themselves in their efforts to make them comfortable. They were just naturally friendly, with the gift of treating people as individuals.

After church on Sunday morning, Colonel MacLeod was in conference with Mrs. Vassilou and David on the subject of the last purchase of wine for the Hermes and, with Josie playing with Prince and some other children from the hotel, Irene found herself alone with Amaranth MacLeod.

She was not, herself, in a very talkative mood. That letter from Guy, which should have been so easy to answer with a quick and loving, 'Yes; I'll marry you most willingly,' was a source of confusion and worry, more than of joy. Was it because, having once made up her mind firmly that marriage with him was out of the question, she found it hard to alter her sights?

At any rate she was glad to be able to let the burden of conversation rest on Amaranth, who thoroughly enjoyed a cheerful chat. The older woman talked chiefly of days gone by, when she and Irene's mother were young – and very lively, it seemed. Their relatives hadn't been very pleased when they married men from outside the island, but apart from both marriages turning out extremely happy, she herself thought a fresh infusion of blood into the island stock was a very good thing, both for the Greek and Turkish populations.

'Your parents were very proud of you and little Josie – and we have always felt just the same about David. He's a grand fellow, a wonderful son. In spite of your grandmother's jokes about him, I'm sure you must find him pleasant to work with.'

Irene hesitated – just for the fraction of a second. Then she said, as warmly as she could: 'He's a very kindhearted person. Just because he thought Josie was lonely, with so few playmates around, he bought her that lovely puppy.'

But Amaranth had noticed that tiny, pregnant pause.

'Maybe David seems a shade forbidding at times, but so did my husband when I first married him. But because we've been so happy together – for I could see through to

142

his real, lovable self – he's relaxed and genial now, as you must have noticed.'

Irene nodded. 'You're dears, both of you,' she said impulsively. 'Easier to understand than David – if you don't mind my saying so!'

'Of course I don't mind. I know very well how edgy he can be. A lot of it can be put down to that horrible accident of his.'

Irene looked at her with a question in her eyes.

'I've known that there *was* an accident, which left him with that slight limp, but no one ever speaks of it. I haven't the faintest idea what happened. I suppose it occurred at sea.'

'Ironically it didn't. He was coming to join us for a holiday in Skye – the island where the MacLeods come from – and was taking a short cut through one of the poorer districts of Glasgow one evening when he nearly shot past a house on fire. The fire brigade hadn't arrived, but there was a child at a window. He jumped out of the car, dashed up the staircase, but it gave way and he was badly burnt. The firemen were there within seconds – rescued him and some other people. But the child he had tried to save was suffocated, dead when they reached her, poor scrap.'

'What a terrible thing!'

'It was the all too frequent case of an immigrant family, too poor to use anything but a cheap, old-fashioned oil heater – and too unused to any heating appliances to manage them properly. It was left in a draught, while the grown-ups were mostly out shopping; and that was that!'

'I suppose David was in hospital for quite a long time.'

'Indeed yes – in Glasgow, at first; then after we'd returned here down in Southampton. We're intensely proud of him. After all, he risked his life for that poor little child. But people are illogical. His failure to save her has always nagged at him. And then, too, having to leave the sea – which was his whole life – was very hard to bear.'

Irene did not speak at first. Then she said quietly: 'Poor David!'

'My dear, don't you ever let him know I've told you. He can't bear to think people are talking about it. As for showing him a grain of sympathy—'

Again Irene was silent. 'I'll certainly hold my tongue,' she said at last. 'But I shall understand him better now, I think.' And then she asked, nervously almost: 'If the thing is never to be talked about, why did you tell me?'

Now it was Mrs. MacLeod's turn to pause; until she said at last, very slowly: 'I really don't know, my dear – unless it's because you're so like your darling mother, to whom I could say anything, in the sure knowledge of her love and understanding.'

Was it because of this that, a few minutes later, Irene found an equal frankness possible? Mrs. MacLeod had gone on to emphasize the great pleasure it would give her and her husband to have a visit from Irene and Josie.

'We've talked about it ever since you came to Cyprus,' she said, 'and it's time we stopped procrastinating. David tells me that this highly competent Mrs. Cipriani is only away temporarily, through some sort of indisposition. Surely when she comes back, you could pay us a visit – at Josie's half-term, perhaps. With a car of your own, which you can drive yourself, it should be a simple matter.'

'It's not so simple,' Irene told her in a burst of confidence. 'No one but Granny knows yet, but I may not be here by then.' And before the astonished Mrs. MacLeod could question her, she went on to tell her the whole history of her love affair with Guy Cosway, and of its recent development.

'If he'd been as amenable as he is now over this question of Josie, I'd never have come to Cyprus – except on a visit, possibly,' she ended, almost in tears. 'We'd have surely worked out some solution. Now when the difficulties are melting away, with Granny delighted to give Josie a home, and Guy letting me have her for the holidays, I can't make up my mind whether to marry him or not. Crazy, isn't it!'

Mrs. MacLeod squeezed her hand. 'No one can advise you, my dear. Certainly I can't. I'm an interested party, longing to keep you in Cyprus, now I've come across you again – and found you so like your darling mother. All I can say is, don't accept him until you're sure you want to. Give yourself time.'

Irene smiled through her tears. 'That's just what he says, more or less. Well, thank you for your patience with such a silly, nonsensical creature. It's been such a relief to talk to you. I've spoken to Granny, and she says just what you do. But I so hate hurting her.'

Mrs. MacLeod smiled back at her. 'Hearts do heal,' she said.

CHAPTER SEVEN

ALTHOUGH the islanders could, like the British, be secretive enough when so inclined, gossip on smaller matters was the order of the day, and the news soon went round that the Kyria's elder granddaughter was in need of driving lessons. These would doubtless be followed by the purchase of a car, it was confidently predicted. And during the week that followed the MacLeods' departure for Limassol, more than one garage owner in the neighbourhood began angling for the order.

'Very premature they are in their hopes,' was Mrs. Vassilou's comment to Irene, when the two found themselves together in the office. 'David wants me to go ahead. He's seen the very car for you, he says – tried it out, what's more. But if you're leaving us and marrying this man, Guy Cosway, it won't be needed.' She paused. 'Could we explain that to him, do you think? Then he'll stop treating me as a dilatory old woman.'

Irene, pale these last few days, went whiter still. 'I'll be coming to a decision very soon now. Could we wait just a little while longer?'

'Of course, if you think it will help. Incidentally I hope you don't mind David helping you to choose the car – if you decide to stay here. He's pretty knowledgeable.'

'I'd be glad if he took full responsibility for the choice. After all, Granny dear, you'll be paying for it. Having him teach me to drive is a different matter altogether.'

'Finding a teacher will be a very easy matter.' Mrs. Vassilou gave a dry little smile. 'But even here I think David should at least have the casting vote. He favours an elder brother of Panos, I believe – another of Nicos' numerous relatives. He worked in a garage at Athens, when the family were living in Greece. Is aiming at a partnership in Kyrenia now.'

'That would suit me very well.' And then she added desperately: 'Oh, Granny, why can't I make up my mind?'

'I suppose you haven't begun to feel interested in another man?'

Mrs. Vassilou was not looking at Irene as she spoke; she was leafing over a ledger. Her voice, too, was casual.

Not so Irene's. She asked in shocked tones: 'How could I – with Guy still loving me?'

'Easily, my dear child! That Mr. Nikolaides – Andreas is his Christian name, isn't it? – is a very handsome and attractive person. He hasn't been around quite so much lately, but if you gave him the least encouragement he'd be on the doorstep.' And she added lightly: 'To be loved is one thing. To love is another. If you returned Guy Cosway's love, would there really be a problem for you?'

This time Irene did not answer the old lady's question. 'Oh, *Granny*!' she said, and went to her typewriter to deal with the morning's mail.

A little later that morning when she was in the grounds, chatting with Hector, the head gardener, David, came along and asked stiffly if he could have a word with her.

'Of course, if you don't mind coming along to the pantry. I must get these flowers in water quickly.'

'O.K., I shan't keep you a minute.'

When they were alone in the white-tiled pantry, and she began filling the vases for the dining-room, he said shortly: 'As you're so set on avoiding me, I haven't had the chance until now of thanking you for making my parents so welcome. I appreciate it.'

'There's no need to thank me. I try to show courtesy and kindness to all our guests.'

'I thought perhaps you really liked them – as they liked you!'

Her back was turned to him, but she faced him now.

'As a matter of fact I did. So you see, there's even less need for your thanks.' She spoke blandly, even with a slight smile, but he flushed with annoyance.

'Can't we ever have a civilized conversation?' he demanded. 'I can't say a word to you without all your prickles coming up.'

'Are you calling me a porcupine? Last time it was a tiger!'

'A tiger?' He looked at her as though nonplussed. 'You must be dreaming! What did I actually say?' She went scarlet now, and he said with that sudden, amused smile of his: 'Oh, of course. We were talking about kissing.'

She knew very well that he had only pretended to forget that ridiculous remark, but she certainly wasn't going to argue the matter with him. It had been extremely stupid of her to refer to it, but it had just slipped out.

'What do you want to speak to me about?' she demanded chillingly.

'To ask if you mind my helping you choose the car your grandmother's going to give you. I shan't be in the least put out if you'd prefer another adviser. Your friend Andreas Nikolaides probably knows more about foreign cars than I do, having lived in Europe and the States so long.'

'I daresay. But his ideas might be too extravagant. I don't want to run my grandmother into spending a lot of money unnecessarily.'

'You can be sure I wouldn't do that. To come down to brass tacks, shall we proclaim a peace-pact for a few hours, and go to Kyrenia this afternoon to have a look at a find I've made? We could take Miss Taylor and Josie along to that little house we hear so much about, and go on to the garage.'

'That would be very kind. But, David' – she caught her breath – 'I don't want it spread abroad yet – I may be returning to England before long.'

'You mean – on a visit?'

She shook her head. 'No, permanently.'

'I see!' His voice sounded curiously bleak. 'Hard luck on your grandmother and the poor old Hermes.'

'And I'm afraid on Josie, too. By the way, I don't want the kid to hear anything about it yet.'

'Are you talking about me?' Josie came running in. 'What is it I mustn't hear? I hope there's nothing wrong!'

It was David who saved the situation.

'My dear, you have a birthday soon, haven't you? Perhaps we're discussing a special treat for you!'

After a momentary look of doubt the child's face cleared. She reached up to hug him, and he swung her off her feet and kissed her.

'Uncle David, I do love you!' she exclaimed. Then, breaking free, she ran across to Irene: 'Not quite so much as you. I'll never love anyone else that much. But he and Granny, they're beginning – *just* beginning – to catch up.'

Later, however, when she was helping Irene carry the vases to the dining-room, she said something which Irene found disquieting.

'I'm glad it was just about my birthday that you and Uncle David were talking. I know it's silly. But sometimes I still get a little scared. And when I heard you say "the kid mustn't hear"—'

Irene smiled down at her reassuringly. 'And now – you're happy?'

'Mostly I am. Only last night I dreamt I was back

148

with Aunt Ethel in Maida Vale, and you were still here with Granny. I was crying a little when I woke up, but kept very quiet so as not to disturb you.'

They had reached the dining-room, now, empty but for a couple of waiters setting out tables for lunch, and handed over their first consignment of vases.

Then Irene said: 'I have silly dreams myself sometimes. I just don't take any notice of them. You know there's a saying: "Dreams go by opposites".'

'That would mean your being with Aunt Ethel, and my staying with Granny, I'd hate that — thinking all the time of Aunt Ethel being cruel and unkind to you!'

Irene managed to laugh. The thought came into her head then that here was the moment to test Josie's reactions to the idea of her marriage with Guy — speaking of it in the lightest way as a mere possibility. But she couldn't bring herself to do it. Not, strangely enough, from a streak of moral cowardice. But because she suddenly knew with blazing certainty that for some reason which she could not, would not face, she no longer wanted to marry Guy, would never do so.

After dinner that night she told her grandmother of her decision. Mrs. Vassilou, upright in her high chair, nodded slowly.

'I guessed it would work out like that,' she said quietly. 'And I'm very sure that with the whole position differing so much from last Christmas, it's not Josie's welfare that's now making you say "No" to this man. Josie's happiness is secure, bound as she would be to miss you at first if you went to England. You've been able to make a free choice — which is just as it should be.'

'You're right, Granny. If I'd loved Guy still, I shouldn't have been tormented over how to act.' She hesitated. 'I hate hurting Guy, but I'm sure he won't be very long in finding another girl — one without problems.'

'And possibly you'll find another man yourself,' was Mrs. Vassilou's calm rejoinder. 'There are many attractive men in Cyprus who would make good husbands. You've only met a fraction of them yet.' She smiled a little. 'In the villages here they still go in for match-makers. It has its points, you know.'

Irene returned her smile. 'When I've written a letter to Guy and posted it,' she said firmly, 'I shall feel free. And that is how I want to be.'

Indeed, once her letter – sweet but definite – had gone off in the mail, she felt that a weight had been lifted from her heart. She could live serenely now in the present, with neither past regrets nor future problems to disturb her.

She accepted now that invitation which David had given her, to go to Kyrenia with him and inspect what he believed was just the car for her – at a bargain price. And a little later in the week saw them starting off on this quest, with Miss Taylor and Josie sitting happily in the back of David's car.

They drove first to the little house which Miss Taylor had now arranged with the lawyers to rent on a yearly basis, dropped her there with Josie to await the arrival of some excellent second-hand furniture she had recently bought.

'We'll have some tea for you when you come back from the town,' Miss Taylor promised, and Josie, hopping about like a sparrow, added that she would take them on a tour of exploration over the house and garden.

Alone with Irene in the car, setting out now on the final mile or so to Kyrenia, David remarked that, since they were observing a peace pact, he hoped it was in order to tell her that he was very glad she was staying on with her grandmother.

'She would have missed you far more than she would have ever acknowledged,' he added – careful, it seemed, to rob his words of any personal flavour. 'Your mother's death, and then her husband's – the loss of the two most important people in her life – left her a very lonely person, for all her friends and relatives.'

'We were pretty lonely, too, after our parents died, living in London with an aunt who resented us.' Her face was sombre now. 'I sometimes feel I can never forgive her for what she did to Josie.'

'You don't mean she was physically cruel to the child?' he demanded sharply.

'Oh, no! Just treated her as a damned nuisance. Yet she was furious when we came away. Missed the money, I suppose.'

'I can appreciate that Josie must have been lonely. But you shouldn't have suffered in that way, surely. Even before this man Guy came on the scene, wanting you to marry him, there must have been others. I don't want to flatter you, or any nonsense like that, but you must be well aware that you're a very beautiful young woman, and extremely attractive to most men, anyway.'

'If not to you,' she thought dryly, and observed that the peace pact must be indeed elastic to allow him to utter such polite remarks.

Their conversation was cut short now by their arrival at the garage, where Irene was introduced first to Spyridon, the stout, smiling proprietor, and then to the neat little Hillman which David had found for her.

'Take the young lady for a quick drive, Kyrie Mac-Leod,' Spyridon suggested. 'You have tried it out, I know, but we must have her opinion, too.'

'If that elder brother of Panos is around – Neo, they call him, I think – he had better take her. She needs lessons, and I understand Neo is a good and experienced teacher.'

'He is indeed – clever, like all that family, and more responsible than young Panos. I knew the lot of them before they went to Greece. Can't think why they didn't stay there.' And he disappeared into a back region and bellowed: 'Neo! Kyria Vassilou's granddaughter is waiting here. Come at once!'

Neo – named after a Cypriot-born saint, Neophitis, it appeared – was an older edition of Panos, and seemed delighted at the idea of teaching Irene to drive. He must have a quick wash and change his coat, he insisted, before taking her out in the Hillman, but while Spyridon was still pointing out the beauties of the 'highly desirable' car, he reappeared, positively dapper-looking, and ushered her into the seat next the driver's with typically Cypriot courtesy. He made this trial run a brief lesson, and by the end of it, when they were back in the garage, she was able to tell the waiting David that both the car, and the tutor, suited her admirably.

'Fine,' he said, with evident relief at her prompt decision. 'We'll take delivery, Spyridon, as soon as possible. Then Miss Meredith will arrange with Neo the times of her lessons. She's a very busy young lady, you know, working hard at the Hermes.'

Amid bows and smiles they set out now for the cup of tea which Miss Taylor had offered them and for Josie's promised tour.

A small quantity of furniture had been delivered during their absence, and some chairs and a small table had been dusted by their hosts, and arranged to the best possible advantage on the veranda.

But Irene was far more interested in the cottage itself than in the refreshments provided. She did not wonder now why it so fascinated Josie – and so pleased Miss Taylor. A small, whitewashed building, backing on to open country, it stood less than a hundred yards away from a handsome brick mansion in front of which a couple of cars were standing and a dog, of the same breed as Prince, lay drowsing.

'I can understand the cottage suiting Miss Taylor,' David remarked as they drove up to it. 'She'll have the privacy here which means so much to her, yet neighbours within call. If the children want to make a noise they can go straight up on the hillside. They won't disturb anybody.'

'And it's so pretty,' Irene exclaimed, looking entranced at the unfenced garden which surrounded the little house. 'It must have been a picture here, earlier in the year, before the heat spoiled all the flowers.'

'It was indeed.' Miss Taylor, came out of the front door as David and Irene reached the veranda. 'I had friends living here fairly recently, and in spring their massed geraniums and huge, glorious carnations were out of this world. I mean to have it just as beautiful here – though I haven't their lovely furniture and hangings.'

'I think your furniture's very nice, Miss Taylor,' Josie declared, following the old lady out. And she told the others with that funny little air of importance that Irene, at least, found touching: 'We haven't got straight yet, except for the heaviest things, which the men put where Miss Taylor told them. I'm pretty strong; but I'd be more help if I were taller.'

'She's been a great help,' Miss Taylor assured Irene and David. 'But in any case, there's a lot more stuff to come next week. Josie and I,' and she laid her hand on the child's shoulder in an affectionate gesture, 'haven't chosen the best rugs yet. And now, dear, will you make the tea for us? The kettle's on the boil.'

Irene felt a deep pleasure sitting out on the sunny little veranda, with the other three. David seemed more tranquil, more at ease, than ever before – or at least since that golden afternoon, at Bella Pais, the old monastery, perched perilously on its high crags – and silent but for the cries of swallows and swifts as they soared and swooped in the cloudless sky.

Not that there was silence now. Josie, for one, was full of chat. Had Irene and Uncle David noticed that lovely dog lying outside the big house? Well, it was a lady, and only two years old, and if the people living there, who seemed very nice, wanted some lovely puppies some time – well, what about Prince being the father?

'He's a bit young for marriage at present,' David observed, smiling.

'Oh, I know. But later on, when he's quite grown up. Miss Taylor says I can come and spend a weekend sometimes when she's settled down here, and that I can bring Prince. So you see they could get to know each other!'

'You've romantic ideas.' It was David who spoke again, still amused at the little girl's enthusiasm.

'Oh, it's not just that,' Josie assured him seriously. 'You can sell puppies, and make a lot of money.'

None of the grown-ups thought it necessary to set her

to rights on the financial side of dog-breeding, and the conversation moved to a more immediate transaction – the purchase of the car for Irene's use, and a schedule of lessons. It was a matter in which they all had a direct interest, and Irene, a little perturbed by so much enthusiasm had to point out that she might have a lot of difficulty in passing her test. She had known people in England who had had several attempts, and one, at least, who had never got through.

'That was Aunt Ethel,' Josie averred. 'Her instructor told her she'd never make a driver. But it didn't stop her going into competitions to win a car. If Uncle Herbert wouldn't drive her around, she could always sell it – that's what she said.'

'Very sensible, too,' Miss Taylor told her dryly. 'And I have great sympathy with your aunt – on this point, anyway I can't drive a car, either.'

'Well, it won't matter now.' Josie's eyes were sparkling. 'Once Irene has a car she'll take you here, there and everywhere. Won't you, Sis?'

Irene nodded, and David said good-humouredly, 'I'm sure she will. Meanwhile,' and he glanced at his watch, 'we'd better be moving. And Miss Taylor, if I can help you next week, when the rest of your belongings arrive, I'll be very glad to do so.'

If only he could always be like this, Irene thought, as they piled up in his car for the short run home – kindly, good-natured, and with a sense of fun. Doubtless this was the side of his personality which he invariably showed to Miss Taylor and Josie, and other people he liked. If she herself happened to be around at the same time his pleasant manner might well extend to her.

Not, however, when they were alone. They would have a short peace pact, he had said. But surely between sensible adults a surface amiability could be maintained indefinitely. Antagonisms might well remain. No amount of effort could make two people like each other. But common courtesy should not be beyond their power to achieve. And tact, so that they did not continually rub each other up the wrong way.

In the weeks that followed they did, indeed, quarrel less. But then they were seeing less of each other.

Once Irene started her driving lessons with Neo, in the new little Hillman, Mrs. Vassilou insisted on taking over much of her work at the Hermes. The sooner she obtained her licence the better: she mustn't be handicapped by tiring herself in other ways. Driving on the mountainous Cyprus roads was no picnic, as she would very soon find.

Neo proved an excellent teacher. In contrast with Panos, his young brother, he was quiet in his manner, saying little beyond what was absolutely necessary. But one day, going through Kyrenia, and stopping for a woman with a shopping basket to cross the road, he observed disdainfully: 'That Mrs. Cipriani, she wouldn't demean herself to say thank you.'

Irene, who had also recognized Delphine, shot him a look of surprise. 'Perhaps she didn't notice you,' she observed pacifically.

He gave a short laugh. 'She takes good care not to see me or any of my family,' he told her.

'I know that she and Panos don't hit it off!'

He sniffed. 'She would get him sacked if she could. It is only our relationship with Nicos that protects him, for she is a very clever liar.'

'But even if she doesn't like Panos, why should she extend this feeling to you?'

'It is our immediate family that she detests.'

'But why?' She avoided with dexterity a car on the wrong side of the road, and won a nod of appreciation from him.

Then he said, with a shrug: 'Because we were living in Greece a while ago in the street where she herself had a flat. Does she think we went there to spy on her? We were in that street before she came – and we returned to Kyrenia at least a year before she did.'

'You knew her there?' Irene was half ashamed of her

curiosity. But it seemed such a ridiculous situation.

'Naturally we met in the market. But we never ex-changed a word. She was too forbidding – didn't even like it if we smiled at her pretty baby.' He hesitated. 'My mother was sorry for her – she seemed to have no friends. But she wouldn't risk a snub.'

And then, as though ashamed of his talkativeness, he gave a deprecating smile, and remarked very politely: 'But we must concentrate on our lesson, Miss Irene. Kyria Vassilou is sure you will pass your test in record time. We mustn't disappoint her.'

Irene smiled back at him, 'How right you are, Neo.' And while she was on the road, practising starting and stopping, she kept her attention fixed, of necessity, on what she was doing.

But later that day, in siesta time, as she lay out on her balcony, she could not prevent her thoughts straying to what Neo had said – to wondering what lay behind Del-phine's rather strange behaviour. Or was there, perhaps, a fairly obvious solution to the problem?

CHAPTER EIGHT

SHORTLY after Irene passed her test with flying colours, Mrs. Vassilou reminded her that Delphine's exile – or leave of absence as she would doubtless prefer to call it – was ending.

She herself had almost forgotten. Not so David. He had been in touch with her, found her anxious to return, and was making a special trip into Kyrenia to fetch her. What was more, Delphine, acting strangely out of character, had petitioned to be allowed to bring Theo along with her.

He was looking white and peaked, and his appetite had fallen off. A month at the Hermes, during which time she would try to coach him a little in her spare time, would make all the difference to him.

'It's a pity I can't take him down with Josie to Miss

Taylor's new little school,' Irene remarked thoughtfully. 'There'd be no question there of his overworking – and it would save him falling back too far. His present school wouldn't mind, surely. And Miss Taylor doesn't know the meaning of red tape.'

Mrs. Vassilou shook her head.

'Delphine has quite a few bees in her bonnet,' she returned. 'She doesn't like Josie and Theo spending a lot of time together. In fact, the knowledge that Josie is bound to be out most of the day has influenced her, I think, in asking us to let her bring the boy here.'

'They'll get together, all the same, those two,' Irene prophesied, smiling. 'And though I can't pretend I shall be rejoiced to have Delphine back again, I'm delighted for Josie's sake that Theo is coming. She's missed him a lot, poor scrap.'

And indeed both children were thrilled to be together once more. Theo had been allowed to bring his own puppy who, with Prince, soon began to figure in exciting make-believe games. The old gardening shed – their 'secret place' – came into its own again, and no efforts on Delphine's part could keep Theo from rushing to join Josie, once Irene had brought her back from the new little school.

With David avoiding her, and showing an inclination for Delphine's company, Irene found herself missing Andreas. It was tiresome having to be on one's guard with a man. Still, he was gay and amusing. It would have been pleasant to see him occasionally. But since that night of the ball, he had made no move to get in touch with her.

More than once, while Neo was giving her a lesson in coping with the Nicosia traffic, she had caught a glimpse of him. But either he didn't see her, or didn't wish to, and she came to the conclusion that he must be deeply offended with her for allowing David to usurp his privilege and drive her home.

It wasn't, she told herself crossly, that she was the kind of girl who must have masculine society. She wasn't as silly and vain as that. In any case many of the young men who came to the Hermes put out friendly feelers: would have been glad to take her around in her off time, and she had turned them down with one excuse or another.

No, she really didn't know what was wrong with her. When she had first sent that letter definitely refusing Guy, she had experienced a sense of relief – of freedom. Now she felt restless and depressed – and ashamed of being in this state.

Mrs. Vassilou, too sharp-eyed to miss Irene's moodiness, try as she might to hide it, came to the conclusion that she was suffering from reaction over this business of Guy Cosway. She didn't believe that the girl regretted her decision not to marry him. But to turn him down altogether after their close friendship, now that his attitude to Josie had so changed for the better, must have been a great ordeal, especially as she had no interest, it seemed, in any other man.

A change of scene was what the girl needed, she decided, and within a few days of Delphine's return, Irene and Josie were starting off in the Hillman on the road to Limassol in fulfilment of a renewed invitation from the MacLeods to pay them a visit.

Although she was pretty sure that her grandmother was behind this last cordial letter from Amaranth, she was very ready to co-operate. She had found Delphine as difficult as ever, and longed to be out of her orbit.

Josie's only regret was leaving Theo behind. In spite of Delphine's subtle efforts to keep the two children apart, they had outwitted her at every turn, and in view of Mrs. Vassilou's approval of the friendship, she could take no drastic action. Now the little boy was under her complete control. He must be content to play with his puppy, under her strict, maternal eye.

What David thought about this visit to his parents, Irene did not know. He sent them pleasant messages, rigged up a comfortable cage affair for Prince, from which he could not escape to harass the driver, and stood by the car with Mrs. Vassilou to speed them on their way.

It was a long drive, and both Josie and the dog were asleep for much of the time. But at last they came to the outskirts of the busy port and following a pencilled map which Amaranth had sent them, reached the low white house which was their destination.

The MacLeods' welcome was heart-warming. Although they had stopped sometimes on the way, to eat the picnic meals which Chef had provided for them, it was a very long trip: by far the longest that Irene had yet undertaken. She was very tired, and deeply thankful to arrive. After a light but delicious meal the two girls turned in, to fall asleep, to the faint scent of dried carob beans – a scent which they were later to find was characteristic at this time of year of all the island's southern ports.

The next day was given up to resting – sitting on the wide verandas, chatting with Amaranth. She had plenty to tell them of the history of this part of Cyprus, centring on the ruins of old Limassol five miles away: plenty to say, too, of the present port's multifarious activities, with all manner of ships in and out of the harbour, carrying on the trade of centuries all over the blue Mediterranean. But always she came back to the subject nearest her heart – David – though apologizing sometimes for being a bore.

Josie, hearing this remark, stopped grooming Prince for a moment and looked up reproachfully.

'But, Aunt Amaranth, we love Uncle David – don't we, Irene? He's such a kind person. You know,' and her blue eyes were round, 'we couldn't have brought Prince if he hadn't fixed that open kennel for him at the back of the car. Everyone had been saying it wouldn't be safe to take such a young dog all this way. Irene's a very good driver, but if Prince had started jumping around—'

'He is a very considerate person.' Amaranth's eyes were soft. 'Just like my husband. Fond of children, too.'

Josie nodded enthusiastically. 'Everyone in Cyprus seems to like children,' she observed happily. 'Except perhaps Mrs. Cipriani.'

'That's ridiculous, dear,' Irene shook her head at her. 'She's very fond of Theo, even if she seems rather strict with him.'

'Well, she doesn't like me – and I don't like her,' Josie returned obstinately. And she asked Mrs. MacLeod frankly: 'Do you like her, Aunt Amaranth? Uncle David does, though I can't think why.'

'We can't all like the same people, darling,' was Mrs. MacLeod's easy reply. 'We've seen very little of her. And when we do meet, she seems very pleasant. I know David thinks very well of her work at the Hermes.'

Josie, tiring of grown-up conversation, wandered off just then, and Amaranth remarked haltingly: 'I don't much care for that Cipriani woman myself, but David says she's a very good sport. She seems to have behaved very decently to you, Irene dear, over that rather serious mistake you made, soon after your arrival at the Hermes.'

'Serious mistake?' Irene stared at her in bewilderment. 'What on earth does she mean?'

'Forgetting to deal with some important letter from Stockholm, making a booking for a party of young Scandinavians. She wouldn't have mentioned it to him, if the Stockholm office hadn't furnished him with proof, several weeks later, that their letter had actually been delivered at the Hermes on the date stated.'

Irene eyed Amaranth steadily.

'This is very interesting. What else did she say?'

'That you were so upset when the tourists arrived and found they weren't expected that you lost your head and tore up the letter – which was in a drawer of the office all the time. She felt very sorry for you. But you pulled yourself together so well over helping her to get the party fixed up with beds and meals, she hadn't the heart to give you away. There didn't seem any point in it either. Once the tourists were comfortably accommodated, the incident seemed to be closed.'

Irene hesitated. Should she come out with the true story? Would Amaranth, who after all didn't know her well, necessarily believe her? Trying to control her ridiculous trembling, she said as evenly as she could, 'It wasn't quite like that. I'd rather not talk about it now. But if you don't mind, I'll take it up with David and my grandmother as soon as I go home.'

Amaranth nodded. 'If she's not telling the truth – in every particular – that's just what you should do,' she told her. 'I must say that, for myself, I'd trust your word far more than Mrs. Cipriani's. And if David has any sense, he will, too. She's pretty enough, but her eyes are shifty – though my husband scolds me for saying so.' She gave an expansive sigh. 'My dear, aren't men fools – but what should we do without them?'

Irene's indignation was so great at this revelation of Delphine's contemptible conduct, she had the utmost difficulty in behaving normally. Disgusted over Delphine's lies, hurt and angry with David for believing them, she was forced to exercise an iron self-control over herself for the sake of her hosts and Josie. The visit was intended to give pleasure to all four of them: she mustn't wreck the little holiday by giving way to her outraged feelings. Time enough for that when she was back at the Hermes, confronting Delphine and David with this travesty of the facts.

Try as she might, she could not herself enjoy the holiday.

Eager to show their guests the activities of this thriving sea-port, the centre of the island's flourishing wine trade, the MacLeods confined their attention first to Limassol itself. Colonel MacLeod seemed to know innumerable people not only in his own line, the wine trade, but in other important enterprises. Some of his friends were engaged in the export of those strangely smelling carob beans – 'black gold' they were called because of the wealth they brought to Cyprus through their myriad uses – ending up, the girls learnt, not merely as cattle food, but as building materials, face cream and goodness knew what.

But of course to Colonel MacLeod the production and sale of the glorious island wines meant everything. And listening to him talking of this vintage and that with his friends in the trade, Irene's mind flew back to those meals in London restaurants with Guy, his disdain for any table wine that did not come directly from France or, preferably, Germany. She had learnt a lot since those days, she reflected, and not only about wine or even hotel-keeping. About human nature!

At their evening meal one night, struck by her host's intense interest in all matters concerning wine, she asked the MacLeods how it was that David, after being invalided from the British Merchant Navy, hadn't joined his father's firm.

'There didn't happen to be a suitable opening at the time,' Colonel MacLeod explained. 'But apart from that he really wanted a post where he could organize and direct some particular enterprise. That, he felt, was what his training as a ship's officer had fitted him for. So when your grandparents' offer came along, he took it. We were thrilled. He might so easily have taken a job outside Europe, even. In America, perhaps, where there seem so many opportunities for capable people.'

'I'm glad he went to the Hermes,' Josie observed enthusiastically, looking up from her soup. 'So is Granny. Our grandfather thought it would take a long time to train him, but it didn't. He was a very quick learner.' She glanced across at her sister with pride. 'So is Irene. Everyone says so.'

The smile which Irene gave her was rather an odd one, but Josie, absorbed again in her supper, did not notice it. She at least, Irene reflected, was enjoying her holiday.

Invitations began to come in now to the MacLeods, for their young relatives, but acceptances had to be cut down to a minimum.

'You must come back in October, for the Wine Festival,' Colonel MacLeod told them. 'There'll be plenty of junketings then. But on this, your very first visit, we must see that you imbibe some history, and take you to Amathus, the original Limassol, five miles away.'

Josie's eyes lit up at this. 'Miss Taylor's taught us about

the old Limassol. It's where Richard Coeur de Lion married the beautiful Princess Berengaria, after all sorts of exciting adventures. Just like a fairy tale.'

Colonel MacLeod smiled down at her.

'We'll go tomorrow,' he said. 'Make a picnic of it.'

But the next day brought a surprise. David telephoned very early to say he was coming to spend the day with them – was already well on his way. Kyria Vassilou, he told his mother with slight amusement, had said he could well be spared for a few hours – had even insisted that when the opportunity occurred, it was his filial duty to visit his parents.

The MacLeods were of course delighted, and young Josie was radiant. As for Irene, the anger she had been feeling towards David was coloured with sheer nervousness of being in his company at all.

She was unlikely to have much chance of speaking to him about those lies of Delphine's – but how could she behave naturally with him while smothering her resentment? Why, oh, why must he come?

It was fortunate, perhaps, that she had so little time for working herself up into a fever of apprehension. At ten o'clock he was driving his car to the gate, and coming up the garden path to hug his mother and Josie, shake hands with his father in British fashion and, in Cypriot mode now, drop a light kiss on Irene's cool fingers.

His big car, and the absence of traffic on the roads for much of the way, had made his journey an easy one, and after he had breakfasted, he was all set to accompany them to Amathus.

In her agitated mood, much of the interest and beauties of the ancient ruins were lost on Irene. She found David's presence extremely disturbing, and though she hated to admit it, was not only angry with him, but deeply hurt. She tried hard to avoid being alone with him, but Amaranth, who had missed nothing of the unrest that had possessed the girl since that fateful conversation, managed things so cleverly that in the late afternoon, David and Irene found themselves finishing a stroll alone, the others having returned by a shorter route to the car.

'Thank God we're on our own for a minute or two,' David exclaimed at once. 'I've been trying to get you to myself ever since I came, pretty well. What's the matter, for goodness' sake?'

Her colour rose. 'I wasn't going to speak of it until I was back at the Hermes. But as you're here you may as well learn what I think of you.'

He stopped in his tracks. 'I gather that I shall hear nothing very favourable. But that hardly surprises me.'

'It shouldn't. When I tell you that your mother, not sharing your touching admiration for Delphine, put me wise about a few lies told about me – and taken by you as gospel!'

'Go on,' he said quietly.

She tried to speak collectedly, but couldn't. And out came the story as told her by Amaranth – the story, false in every detail, that she had not only been guilty of great carelessness over an important letter from Scandinavia – carelessness that might have given them a very bad name with Swedish travel agents. That she had tried to cover herself up by destroying the letter in Delphine's presence, ready to lie herself out of any future inquiries.

'Delphine did tell me that, but begged me not to report it to Kyria Vassilou. She was sorry for you, she said, didn't want your grandmother to think badly of you. I – I felt sorry for you, too. After all, you were inexperienced, I wasn't at all shocked at your giving way to panic.'

'How very kind of you! And I gather you thought it sporting of Delphine not to spread the story abroad. Well, now you're going to hear the truth and I don't care a damn whether you believe me or not. It was Delphine who forgot that letter – she was all nerves at the time – and when I came across it and showed it to her she snatched it out of my hand and tore it up into small pieces.'

He stopped in his tracks. 'Irene, how could I have been such a fool?'

'Then you accept my version?'

'Of course I do! Now I know you better I realize that moral cowardice is not one of your faults, that you employ a disconcerting frankness.'

'Why didn't you put it right – with your mother, for instance?'

'Because, believe it or not, I'd practically forgotten the whole silly episode. After all, what did it matter the letter from Stockholm being torn up, once the tourists had arrived?'

'How did the Swedes prove that the letter had reached the hotel?'

'Because on the day it arrived Hercules signed for it. As you may possibly remember he was away ill at the time of that unexpected invasion, and anyway he doesn't scrutinize the correspondence.'

She did not speak for a moment. Then she said: 'I suppose it's petty of me to mind so much. But I can't help it. I do!'

'I can only tell you I'm desperately sorry. But I'd known Delphine so much longer than you, instinctively sympathized with her.'

'Still do, no doubt. You're going to marry her, aren't you?'

'If I had ambitions in that direction I should be very cast down just now. She's been going around just lately with someone a good deal more sprightly than myself.'

'I don't understand you,' she exclaimed. 'I never shall.'

'But you'll accept my grovelling apology? It doesn't come easy to me to eat humble pie, you know!'

'Of course I accept it. And please, let's hurry up and join the others.'

He shrugged his shoulders indifferently. 'As you please. There certainly seems nothing else to say,' adding suddenly, before they started hurrying off: 'At the moment, anyway – Miss Meredith!'

Within a very few minutes they had caught up with the MacLeods and Josie – walking in silence, though every now and then David took her arm firmly to help her over a difficult patch of rocky path.

His touch increased her unrest, bringing her feelings she shrank from acknowledging even to her inmost self, but which would not be denied. Stronger than anger and resentment, overwhelming them indeed, were the tremors that shot through her. Primitive, passionate tremors, betraying feelings she had tried for weeks to ignore.

She had thought that her affection for Guy Cosway was love. But, dear God, what had it in common with these surgings of passion, of utterly senseless tenderness?

Using every ounce of will-power she did her utmost to conceal the turmoil which possessed her, and he, too, behaved as though that stormy conversation had not taken place. Easier by far for him, she thought, to show calmness. He had no emotions to keep in check beyond annoyance.

When he had gone, blowing kisses to his parents and to Josie, and those who were left were sitting in the Mac-Leods' pleasant house, talking over the exciting and interesting things they had seen at old Limassol, Mrs. MacLeod produced a note which David had brought her from Kyria Vassilou. If she thought Irene and Josie would like the idea, would she make arrangements for them to break the journey to the north coast by staying a couple of nights en route at Platres, the mountain resort in the Troodos range. Going up into the mountains would, of course, increase the mileage, but to divide it in this way would greatly lessen the fatigue.

'Your grandmother has great faith in your skill as a driver,' Amaranth told Irene, 'and of course the roads are pretty good. But David doesn't approve, says it will be too much of a strain on you — left my husband and me to do the arguing — which I told him was a very ungracious way of putting it.' While Josie hopped around excitedly Colonel MacLeod came into the room, and his wife asked him what he thought of Kyria Vassilou's idea.

'Grand — with modifications,' he returned good-humouredly. 'We'll four of us go to Platres next weekend. We'll have to take the two cars, of course. I'll book rooms right away.'

His wife was so delighted she went up and kissed him.

'It gives us a heaven-sent excuse for getting a whiff of mountain air,' she said. 'You'd like to go, Irene, wouldn't you?'

'Anything,' Irene thought, to avoid being in contact with David — and Delphine — while she was in her present mood. And she said, conjuring up a brilliant smile: 'It sounds the most marvellous idea.'

Indeed it was a wonderful experience climbing up into the Troodos mountains — far loftier than even the impressive Kyrenia range, though less craggy and lacking the high-perched castles with their air of legend. The slopes were covered with fragrant pine forests, and here and there was a barn-like wooden church. As for the air, it was like champagne: it gave the sense of having climbed into a different world.

The hotel, one at which the MacLeods always stayed on their visits to Platres, not only provided every comfort, but made the party hearteningly welcome. There was no formality — less even than at the Hermes. They might have been the proprietor's dearest friends. For two days they stayed there, exploring the wooded hills and valleys, and then it was time for Colonel MacLeod to get back to his office, and for Irene and Josie to continue their journey to Kyrenia, and on to the Hermes.

And then the accident happened. At a wayside garage, a new and enthusiastic helper, who had been ordered strictly to do nothing without supervision, decided to fill up Irene's petrol tank on his own. The result, when the girls came to collect the Hillman, was disaster. The boy had found a can at the back of the car and decided to use it first, before bothering about the petrol pump. And the can had contained water.

Colonel MacLeod, just ready to start back for Limassol, wasted no time on recriminations.

'There's only one thing to do,' he told Irene crisply. 'You and Josie must go back to the hotel and wait for David to collect you. I'll ring him immediately. Even if your car could be put right quickly – and I'm inclined to doubt it – we shouldn't feel happy about your using it straight away. It wouldn't be fair on an inexperienced driver.'

Irene reflected grimly that it wasn't difficult to see where David got his speed at reaching a decision. Both father and son were well capable of playing the martinet.

But she knew in her heart that Colonel MacLeod was right. For Josie's sake, if not for her own, she must avoid the risk of the car coming to grief on one of these mountain roads.

David would hardly be pleased at all this extra driving. He might well make some caustic remarks. But what did she care, anyway? She could always maintain a polite silence, and allow Josie to supply the conversation.

She had been telling herself resolutely that those crazy feelings which had boiled up at old Limassol were sheer nonsense. The influence of the old fertility gods which still haunted the ancient sacred places of the island – that was how modern people would explain it. But the moment she saw him limping towards her late next morning she knew that this rush of passion and tenderness was not something to be laughed away. She could hide it from him – for the shame of showing love unreturned would be unbearable. But she could never change.

He, for his part, was self-possessed and perfectly amiable. All he wanted, for the moment, was a good breakfast, to supplement the cup of coffee he had swallowed, before leaving the Hermes in the early dawn. And while they sat and chatted as he ate it, he told Irene with genuine sympathy that she had suffered incredibly bad luck. It was the kind of thing that happened once in a blue moon.

His breakfast finished, he and Irene, leaving Josie and Prince playing with some children under the proprietor's

168

eye, drove to the garage where the Hillman had been left. He was met by the same vociferous apologies that Irene had already received and, what was more to the point, assurances that the garage owner would himself bring the car back to the Hermes when he could vouch for its being in perfect order. Such a thing had never happened in his little garage before. It brought shame to his business. Everything possible must be done to make amends for that young rascal's folly and disobedience.

There was nothing for it but to collect Josie and Prince and start for home. In the station-wagon there was plenty of room for the three of them to sit in front, Prince being stowed in his 'kennel' at the back. And with Josie the buffer, there was no need for her two elders to engage each other in unnecessary chat.

Somehow, to her surprise, Irene found that she was beginning to enjoy herself. She had been awake much of the night, depressed and humiliated at the thought of David having to push all his work aside and undertake a tiresome 'duty-drive' – of his all too-evident efforts to conceal his annoyance.

But he had reacted quite differently, seemed to regard what might well have been an irritating and boring chore with perfect equanimity, if not mild pleasure.

Apart from Josie's squeaks of excitement when she saw anything unusual, and from David's occasional comments, she could relax and enjoy the wonderful Troodos scenery.

They had a delicious lunch later in the day at a small restaurant, and it was borne in on Irene then that David was, in a quiet way, making every possible effort to please her. And presently, when they were driving through the hot afternoon, and Josie was now asleep in the back of the car, he gave her a clue to his reasons.

'I've been horribly unkind to you, Irene,' he said. 'And I don't mean because I swallowed Delphine's silly story about you. As I told you, I very soon forgot it altogether.'

'I've not always behaved very nicely to you,' she admit-

169

ted. 'But what do you actually mean?'

'I was angry, or I wouldn't have made that remark about Delphine's latest boy-friend.' He hesitated. 'You're bound to hear sooner or later, Irene, who the chap is.'

Self-knowlege struggling in her heart, as it had done more than once in recent weeks, she wondered a shade hysterically what he would have said if she had exclaimed: 'So long as it isn't you who are her sweetheart!' But she controlled herself admirably, and asked coolly: 'Well, who is it?'

'Nikolaides,' was his curt reply. 'I hope you don't mind too much. It's a big surprise to most of us.'

'I don't mind at all,' Irene told him evenly. 'Good luck to them is all I can say. I hope he'll be a kind stepfather to Theo.'

'Cypriots are nearly always kind to children. But I didn't say that there was any question of marriage. It's early days.'

Some stray, elusive thoughts found their way into Irene's brain. Were Delphine and Andreas really such recent acquaintances? Hadn't it seemed to her sometimes that there was an antipathy between them, reaching back into the past?

On and off she puzzled over this on the way home, but when they drove up to Kyria Vassilou's front door at last something happened to put Delphine and Andreas right out of her head.

Josie, running ahead, and calling gaily to her grandmother, stopped dead in her tracks at the open sitting-room door, and gave a sudden, high-pitched wail: 'Irene!'

Startled, and fearing that perhaps Mrs. Vassilou had been taken ill, Irene pushed past the child and flew into the room. Mrs. Vassilou, sitting in her usual stiff-backed chair, wore an almost exaggerated air of calm, as though it was the most natural thing in the world to be entertaining these particular visitors from England.

Uncle Herbert and Aunt Ethel – the former looking embarrassed, the latter jubilant.

CHAPTER NINE

FOR a moment there was silence in the room. Then Mrs. Vassilou exclaimed in her warm deep voice, holding out her arms: 'Welcome home, my darlings,' adding placidly in English, as her grandchildren ran into her arms and kissed her: 'Isn't this a surprise, your aunt and uncle coming to Cyprus?'

Even before she finished speaking, Irene had recovered her self-control, though still feeling as though she had plunged into a nightmare.

'It is indeed,' she said quietly, and went to shake hands with her relatives, followed by Josie, whose small face had become pinched and pale.

David, who had just brought the girls' suitcases into the hall, did not come in to be introduced, but Irene was pretty sure that Aunt Ethel had managed to take a good look at him. Those light-blue eyes of hers seldom missed much.

She was speaking now in a highly elated tone.

'I bet the girls are astonished,' she remarked, beaming, her thin cheeks flushed with excitement. 'But I always knew that if I persevered with these competitions I'd win a decent prize, sooner or later. A fortnight's package holiday, with a choice of three different countries. Well, of course we chose Cyprus.'

Uncle Herbert spoke then, in his usual subdued way.

'I wanted to see you both,' he told Irene and Josie. 'I've missed your presence in the house ever since you left us.' And glancing across at Mrs. Vassilou he went on, smiling rather sadly: 'One misses young things when they go. But they both look well.'

'I wouldn't say that Josie does,' was Aunt Ethel's stiff comment. 'The English climate is better for children of her age! Irene – she doesn't look too bad.'

If Mrs. Vassilou considered her discourteous, she gave

no sign.

She said equably: 'Irene dear, your aunt and uncle were booked to stay at one of the big hotels in Kyrenia. When they rang up from the airport to announce their arrival, I naturally had great pleasure in inviting them to stay at the Hermes instead.'

'I thought the people who run the tour might object, but they didn't at all,' Aunt Ethel observed comfortably. 'So we've arranged to spend one night here now, then go back to join the party and explore the island in all directions, finishing up at the Hermes again for the last day or two.'

'If you are sure we're not trespassing on your hospitality, Mrs. Vassilou?' Uncle Herbert asked the old lady in some embarrassment. 'We had no idea of anything of the kind when we telephoned from the airport this morning.'

Mrs. Vassilou smiled at him. Irene, at least, could tell that she much preferred him to his wife.

'Mr. Meredith,' she said quietly, 'if you knew this cherished homeland of ours, you would be aware that one of our most important words is "*Kopiaste*". It means "Come and join us!" Anyone – a worker, a peasant, a stranger at a coffee-shop – will call out this greeting to you, and expect you to accept the hospitality he offers.'

Aunt Ethel looked affronted.

'You mean, as one goes along the road – a total stranger would call out like that?'

'I do indeed,' Mrs. Vassilou assured her.

Aunt Ethel sniffed. 'Well, I shouldn't like that at all. I'm fussy, I'm afraid.'

'I think it sounds quite heart-warming, Mrs. Vassilou,' Uncle Herbert said quickly. 'My brother – the father of these two girls – told me of Cyprus hospitality. But all the same, we mustn't impose on you.'

For answer Mrs. Vassilou looked at the clock on her mantelpiece.

'Irene dear, Delphine's assigned your relatives a nice bedroom. I suggest you go across and have dinner with them. Josie,' and she slipped her arm round the little girl, 'will stay here and have her usual light supper with me.'

Irene, finding what comfort she could from the fact that within a fortnight her aunt and uncle would be returning to London, resolved to put the best face she could on the situation.

'That sounds an excellent idea,' she said evenly. 'Let's go across now. Say good night, Josie dear!'

Uncle Herbert kissed the little girl, but to the child's hardly disguised relief Aunt Ethel did not follow his example. She gave a nod which included Josie and her grandmother, observed briskly, 'See you tomorrow,' and followed her husband and elder niece over to the main part of the hotel.

Having seen them to their very pleasant bedroom, and arranged to meet them in the restaurant for dinner, Irene made her way to the office, wondering what reception she would get from Delphine. Had David charged her with that lie about the destruction of the Stockholm letter? If so, how had she taken it?

But Delphine was giving nothing away. After making a few gushing remarks about 'your charming English relatives,' she decided that it was nearing Theo's bedtime and that she must go and look for him.

'He spends far too much time with Panos,' she said irritably, as she cleared up her desk. 'Riding on the back of a ramshackle motor-bike, whenever he gets the chance. It's no good my forbidding him' – and now there was bitterness in her voice – 'no one will back me up. I shall be glad, really, when we're back in Kyrenia.'

She was gone before Irene could comment, but David came along just then, in search of a file.

'That must have been a shock to you, Irene,' he remarked. 'Your London relatives turning up without a day's notice!'

'I should say so. It's worse for Josie, though.'

'I'm sure! But she has nothing to be frightened of. They can't kidnap her. Take her back to Maida Vale!'

'Of course not. Aunt Ethel certainly wouldn't want her. But she has a very cruel streak. She's quite capable of teasing Josie – knowing she's scared of her.' She gave a deep sigh. 'If only I had seen Granny before they were in touch with her! I'd have persuaded her not on any account to ask them to stay at the Hermes.'

'It's second nature to your grandmother to show your relatives hospitality, Irene.' David's voice was unusually kind. So much so that Irene asked him impulsively: 'You've been good to me today, David. Could you possibly do something else for me?'

He gave her a slight smile. 'It depends what it is, my dear!'

'You'll think me silly, I know, but Granny's let me in for having dinner with my aunt and uncle. If you could make a four with us, it would make things a lot easier for me.'

He shook his head. 'Sorry, but it's out of the question to join you tonight. Chef's down with 'flu, and I've promised to keep an eye on things in the kitchen. He's left everything in pretty good order, but I'll have to be around.'

Irene tried to smile. 'I wish I could swap with you. My aunt paralyses me when I try to make polite conversation.'

'I know. Some people are like that.' He hesitated, then said a shade awkwardly: 'I suppose you wouldn't feel like asking Delphine along? She seems to have made a hit with them already. Oh, I know she's behaved very badly to you, and all that. But the more one knows of what she's suffered in the past, the more one's inclined to make allowances.'

'She wouldn't come!' Irene told him shortly.

'If I asked her, I'm sure she would. In fact she might like to be invited. She's a funny girl, you know.'

'Well, I'd rather not have her, David. I'll make out all right on my own.'

'I'm sure you will,' was his bland reply. 'If I can find time I'll join you for coffee in the lounge.' And before she could tell him that he need not bother, he had gone striding off in the direction of the kitchen.

She felt very sore, though telling herself that he had behaved precisely as she could have predicted. She well appreciated that, in the circumstances, he could not join her and her relatives at dinner. But why drag Delphine into it? Why was he so soft about her? Why must all her disgraceful behaviour, her lies and discourtesy, be swept under the carpet?

There was only one reason, of course, why, when it came to 'poor little Delphine', all his normal common sense and judgment deserted him. He was more than half in love with her.

As for those hints that she was forming a sudden, rather close friendship with Andreas, he could tell that to the Marines. She didn't believe a word of it. Unless, of course, the idea occurred to her, Delphine was trying the old, old trick. Making David jealous!

Had Irene been alone with her uncle, dinner would have been a pleasant meal, in spite of those troubled and unhappy feelings over David. His knowledge of Greek mythology and of the turbulent history of this exquisite island could have made their conversation intensely interesting. But Aunt Ethel snubbed him at every turn. No one, in her opinion, could want to hear that 'dull old stuff'. Far more exciting and worthwhile in her view was a detailed description of the changes which had turned the house in Maida Vale into two flats – with emphasis on her good taste and clever economies in the choice of bargain-price wallpapers, and dark paint which would show no marks and last for ever.

'All these light decorations you have here are ridiculous,' she declared, looking disapprovingly round the restaurant. 'The china and glass, too – much too fancy. And to tell you the truth,' she pushed some tender lamb and fresh vegetables round her plate – 'I'm not all that stuck on this Greek food. We might have done better – got some plain, sensible English grub, if we'd gone to that big hotel where we were booked in. But we didn't want to offend your grandma.'

From that she went on to opine that Josie's peaky looks were due to the rich cooking, combined with the sultry climate.

'And of course your grandma spoils her! Lets her run wild. No regular schooling for her, I'll be bound.'

'Ethel, you know nothing whatever about it!' Uncle Herbert was stung to speech at last. 'The girls look much happier here than they did in England.'

'They can't be very patriotic, then,' was Aunt Ethel's contemptuous rejoinder. 'Despising their father's country!'

'We loved England when we were living there with our parents,' Irene exclaimed, flushing. 'If they were still alive we might well be there now.'

Which merely brought from Aunt Ethel a sneering and incredulous laugh.

At last the meal came to an end, leaving Irene, at least, extremely tired and dispirited. She wondered, as she led her aunt and uncle into the smaller, cosier lounge, whether David would indeed join them for coffee – and whether he would manage to win even faint approval from Aunt Ethel. Anyway, she would prepare them.

'Mr. MacLeod, our manager, is hoping to come along to meet you,' she told them, leading them to a comfortable corner.

Her uncle made a polite rejoinder, but Aunt Ethel, lighting a cigarette with a flourish, observed that she had been wondering when they were going to be introduced to 'some of your new-found friends'.

Fortunately David came along at that precise moment, and to Irene's surprise and pleasure – and slight amusement – laid himself out to be friendly, taking particular trouble with Aunt Ethel. Never had Irene seen him exercise such charm. And neither, she felt sure, had her grandmother. It was, she had to concede, a remarkable performance.

If Andreas had behaved in that way she would have thought nothing of it. But *David*! She hadn't thought him capable of it. Indeed she would have been slightly shocked at such play-acting, but for the relief of having Aunt Ethel relax into amiability.

Over Turkish coffee, and tiny glasses of Commanderie liqueur, the atmosphere improved still more. But when Aunt Ethel, unused to anything stronger than tea, began to treat David to confidences, Irene, nervous, tried to bring the conversation into more conventional channels.

David, feeling no doubt that he had gone far enough, did his best now to co-operate with her. But Aunt Ethel, in sentimental vein, and sure of his sympathy, was posing happily as the tender and loving-hearted relative who had rushed to the help of her orphaned nieces, and taken them to her heart, never wavered in her affection, in spite of hurtful misunderstanding.

To back this up she produced from her handbag an envelope containing some photographs which she passed across to him – taken mostly by her husband, she explained, with a camera she had won in a competition.

'I'm sure Mr. MacLeod doesn't want to look at these snapshots of Josie and me,' Irene protested.

'I find them most charming and interesting,' was David's polite reply.

Something in his tone, however, startled her, and suddenly noticing the print which he was now examining, she went rigid.

It wasn't a snapshot, nor was it in colour. It was a black and white press picture of herself and Guy taken a year ago, which she had confidently supposed to have been destroyed. A press photographer friend of Guy's had intended to publish it in his paper to coincide with the announcement of their engagement. Before he could do so, the romance had come to an end. But even if it had continued, she would never have agreed to publication and had made this plain to Guy in no uncertain terms.

Posed to the point of crudity – and how she'd disliked the whole sitting – it showed her gazing up adoringly at Guy, who was looking down at her with a sickeningly amorous expression. There was no artistry about it. As she had told Guy – who, astonishingly, had rather liked it – there was only one thing to do with it – put it in the fire.

'Where did you get hold of that wretched thing?' she asked her aunt sharply.

'Guy gave it to me. He carries a copy around. Still hopes, poor fellow.' She sighed. 'I sometimes think that if anyone can lure you back to England it'll be Guy.'

'Isn't all this rather primitive?' David handed the print back to Aunt Ethel, his expression wooden.

'It certainly is. And I've always agreed with Irene as to that print's vulgarity.' Uncle Herbert, with an unusual spurt of courage, snatched the offending photograph from the table and tore it into small pieces.

For a moment it seemed as though Aunt Ethel would fly into a temper, but miraculously she controlled herself, simply giving a contemptuous little laugh.

'I must go.' David got to his feet. 'I've a lot to do before I turn in.' He looked across at Irene, who had stood up too. 'You've some last-minute jobs, too, haven't you?'

Relieved though she was at David's adroit rescue of her, she could find no words in which to thank him. She felt exhausted, humiliated and very unhappy: wanted only to crawl into bed and get to sleep.

'I can't really do any more jobs,' she told him desperately. 'I'm done in.'

'Hard lines!' His tone was still abrupt. 'If you're sensible you'll have a late morning tomorrow. Delphine and I will cope with your relatives, see them off safely.'

'But they'll be coming back here before they go home to England!' Irene looked at him haggardly.

'That doesn't mean the end of the world for you. If your aunt wins another package holiday she won't return to Cyprus, I'm sure. Just as likely to choose Timbuctoo!'

She turned away, absurdly hurt by his apparent lack of sympathy, and at that moment Delphine came along the corridor, pulling on a dust-coat.

'Do you still feel like taking me for a short run?' she

asked David. 'I've been on duty all day, practically non-stop. Unless of course you're changing your mind and taking Irene. Finishing up your sociable evening with a flourish!'

'I'm going straight to bed,' Irene said quickly. 'I've had all the sociabilities I want.' She knew she must sound ungracious, but somehow she couldn't help it.

As she went off she heard Delphine remark lightly: 'What's bitten her now? After all the trouble you've taken!'

But what David answered, she did not hear.

Anxious not to arouse Josie, she undressed very quietly and crept into bed. Once or twice a slight sound made her wonder whether her little sister was as deeply asleep as she appeared, but she told herself that she was imagining things. After a peaceful evening with her grandmother, there was no reason for her to be restless or nervous. She had seen almost nothing of her aunt.

'I wish I could be as placid,' she thought, as she tossed restlessly in the scented darkness. 'No wonder David thinks me a fool, getting worked up over a stupid aunt whom I happen to dislike, and who's leaving Cyprus for good in a matter of days.' And then she demanded of herself fiercely: 'Why should I care a sausage for David's opinion of me? He's nothing to me – never could be. Goodness knows why he doesn't stop shilly-shallying over Delphine and marry her out of hand?'

Brave words! But she couldn't pretend, even to herself, that they rang true. Dour and crotchety as he often was, scornful, impatient, there had been moments when David had shown himself in a far kindlier and gentler light. Fleeting moments when she had felt herself nearer to him than to any human being she had ever known.

That time at Bella Pais, the ruined monastery perched high in the Kyrenia crags, when they had seemed to be caught up in a golden aura of peace and happiness. How close they had come. If only that sense of joy, of complete understanding could have lasted. But it had melted as quickly as a dream. Impossible to believe it would ever return.

CHAPTER TEN

FOR Josie's sake she tried hard next day to hide her weariness of spirit, to appear poised and cheerful. Aunt Ethel's eruption on the scene had come as a great shock to the child, who could still, all too easily, be thrown off balance.

Mercifully the Merediths were gone by the time she got up. They had had to leave after a very early breakfast, David himself driving them into Kyrenia to link up with the rest of their party. It gave her a breathing-space.

Because she had not yet got the Hillman back, she agreed, though not too willingly, to a suggestion from Nicos that Panos should borrow his ancient car and drive Josie to school. Panos was a good driver, Nicos declared, and while she might be nervous at the idea of the child's travelling on the back of his moped, in the car Josie would be perfectly safe.

A grudging permission was extracted from Delphine for Theo to go with them for the ride. And Irene, seeing the children's bright faces, as they whispered together like a pair of monkeys, rejoiced to see Josie pink-cheeked and happy. Those fears which had made her look so white and drawn hadn't lasted. There was no doubt that these peaceful months in Cyprus had given her an underlying sense of security.

A further delay in the return of her car brought a continuation of Panos's duties as chauffeur. To his delight, as well as that of his youthful passengers, it was taken for granted that he should run Josie in and out to school twice a day, and that Theo should go in and out for the drive after lunch, looking in at odd times on his grandmother.

So the days sped by, everyone busy now at the Hermes,

with most of the displaced residents back in their modernized quarters, and Theo, to his great joy, allotted a little room of his own — one which had been part of Miss Taylor's suite.

'If only Aunt Ethel and Uncle Herbert would decide to cut out their farewell visit here,' Irene thought, as the time drew closer for them to make their reappearance.

But no! A telephone call announced their arrival, and she had to get busy preparing the room they had previously occupied, putting fresh flowers in the vases and seeing that all was as spick and span as could be.

On this occasion the Merediths reached the Hermes in time for tea and Mrs. Vassilou, true to her traditions of island hospitality, invited them to come over to taste a sweet cake — *halouvas* — which she had made herself.

And it wasn't enough that Irene should help with the entertaining. Gently but firmly she insisted that Josie, when she returned from school, must put on a clean dress and help pass the cups and plates around. She had seen scarcely anything of her relatives, and this at least she must do.

So Josie came, looking neat and pretty, and though clearly timid, did her best to please her grandmother. She even accompanied her aunt and uncle back to their room after tea without fuss.

But the following day, the Merediths' last in Cyprus, the blow fell. Delphine, answering the telephone at the end of the morning, was informed by Miss Taylor that Josie had not come to afternoon school. She hoped that the child was not ill.

'She was certainly supposed to be going into school,' Delphine exclaimed. 'I saw Panos starting off with her and Theo.'

'Well, perhaps you'll find out what's happened, and let me know. I don't suppose there's anything to worry about. But she's as regular as clockwork as a rule. And it's her favourite subject today: Greek folk-lore.'

Calling to Hercules, the hall porter, to take over the office, Delphine went in search of Irene, determined to give her a piece of her mind. Whatever Miss Taylor chose to say in praise of Josie, she herself considered her a bad influence on Theo, encouraging him in rebellious ways. She had always said so.

But Irene was far too concerned to bother about Delphine's reproaches. The first thing, she declared crisply, was to find Panos and see if he could shed any light on the situation. Josie loved going to school, thought the world of Miss Taylor. It wasn't in character, her playing truant.

Panos, however, who was on the point of going to fetch Josie back to tea, had no explanation to offer. He had dropped Josie, as he always did, quite near Miss Taylor's cottage.

'What about Theo?' Delphine snapped

'I left him at exactly the same place. He said he was going on to look in at his granny's, and would come back and wait, with Josie, at Miss Taylor's, to be picked up at midday.'

'Perhaps he's there, waiting!' Irene suggested. 'Ask Nicos if you can run me in, and I'll look out for the two of them.'

'No need to ask his permission, Miss Irene,' Panos told her stoutly. 'We'll go right away.'

'And for goodness' sake bring Theo back, even if you can't find Josie at once,' Delphine snapped. 'If he's been up to any nonsense I shall know how to deal with him. But he's probably with my mother, still.'

But both at the little school and at Delphine's mother's flat, Irene drew a blank. From the time Panos deposited the children outside Miss Taylor's, soon after lunch, they seemed to have disappeared into thin air. No one had caught sight of them or could provide any clue as to their whereabouts.

After driving round the nearby road, she came back dispirited, but Mrs. Vassilou refused to take the matter seriously.

'They'll turn up when they're hungry,' was her verdict. 'I've played truant myself before now, when I was that age. But it's a pity Josie should disgrace herself while her aunt and uncle are still here. Her aunt already thinks poorly of her Cyprus upbringing, told me flatly yesterday that her father wanted her brought up in England – that she ought to have been left in Maida Vale.' She shrugged her shoulders eloquently. 'What she'll say now, goodness knows.'

David, when he came in from a business interview in Nicosia, was equally sanguine, though sharply annoyed with the trouble which the children were giving. As soon as he could find a moment he would take the station-wagon and have a good hunt for them. They couldn't, he was sure, have gone very far without being spotted. But Irene, going on impulse to visit the old garden shed which Josie and Theo styled their 'secret place,' found fresh cause for anxiety. Several of their 'treasures' had disappeared, including a picnic basket and the shabby lilo, and when she ran to question Panos again he told her, without apparently realizing any particular significance in what he was saying, that for the last few days they had been taking packages in with them – picnic things and so on. Chef often gave them tit-bits. It was only natural when anyone was fond of children to spoil them a trifle.

'Little *wretches*!' was David's verdict, when Irene brought him this last information. But he was so certain of finding them within an hour or two that even Delphine controlled her tendency to hysteria, and contented herself with complaining to everyone who would listen – including Aunt Ethel – that the whole thing was Josie's fault. Theo had been perfectly well behaved until she had come on the scene. She had been a thoroughly bad influence on the boy – younger than herself and naturally timid. She hoped she would be severely punished.

Both girls would have liked to join David in his search, but, at his most dour, he told them shortly that he would prefer to be on his own. And off he went, scowlingly, certain of speedy success.

But hours crawled by, with the Merediths, distinctly uneasy, leaving to catch their plane at Nicosia airport, and no sign of David and the children. And now, darkness falling, anxiety spread throughout the hotel, everyone producing fresh theories. But Irene, sure in her own mind that Josie was hiding from her aunt, for fear she might have arranged to take her back to London, expected any moment that David would bring her back. It was ridiculous. But even a grown-up person, when seized with panic, lost the power to reason.

By midnight hysteria had gripped Delphine.

'I'm telephoning to Andreas,' she told Irene fiercely, as they pottered aimlessly in the office. 'He knows the countryside far better than David does. He lived in the district as a boy.'

Taken aback, Irene could only look at her in astonishment, before observing lamely: 'So it's true, then. That you and Andreas—'

'A lot more is true than you ever imagined,' Delphine snapped, as she seized the telephone. 'Oh, you needn't go. You'll hear everything soon enough.'

In no mind to listen, Irene moved away. That Andreas should join in the search was all to the good. What was between him and Delphine mattered not at all. But she was barely out of earshot when Delphine came running after her.

'He's coming at once,' she gasped. 'Wants to take one of the puppies. He'll find Theo quickly, he swears.'

'That's great of him!' It was the first thing that came into Irene's head. She was nearing the end of her tether, hardly knew what she was saying.

'Wouldn't he do that much for his own child?' came in an outburst from Delphine. 'Now that he knows the truth? Which he's done for weeks past!'

Mrs. Vassilou came wandering in then, looking terribly strained and anxious, and immediately Delphine told her of her call to Andreas.

'Very sensible.' The old lady showed no mystification. 'Irene, most of the servants are still about. Go and get us all some hot soup. And a thermos for Mr. Nikolaides to take with him. The children may be very glad of it.'

Tomato soup – in a thermos! How long ago it seemed, that night at London Airport when Andreas had shown kindness to herself and Josie, and warned her lightly against her grandmother's dour manager. An attractive man; but how little importance he had assumed in their lives.

David! Angry, impatient – unreasonable, as often as not! He was the one who counted. And goodness knew what was happening to him, and the children for whom he was searching.

When Andreas turned up he was in a very different mood from any in which she had ever seen him – quiet, serious, concentrating on the job in hand, but gentle in his manner to Delphine. But he was courteous to Mrs. Vassilou and Irene, too, inviting Irene to join them and Delphine in their quest, and suggesting taking Prince, Josie's puppy, with them.

'He'll only be in the way,' Delphine objected, but Andreas was adamant.

'We'll give him a trial,' he insisted.

But just as they were starting out, the telephone rang again, with the news from Miss Taylor that David was on his way back with the children. And within a few minutes there was the sound of the returning station-wagon.

Theo was out first. Dimly Irene saw him run sobbing into his mother's arms, heard Delphine's broken phrases of affection and reproach as she kissed and caressed him. But the next moment her eyes were on David, lifting Josie, inert and silent, from the car, and carrying her towards her grandmother's apartments.

He was limping worse than she had ever seen him, and when she flew across to him she saw that Josie was deathly white but for a trickle of blood running down her face from her forehead.

'We must get her to bed at once,' David told her. 'But don't worry too much. She's beginning to recover consciousness.'

'But your foot! You ought not to be walking on it. Hercules will carry her, or Panos. Oh, *David*, I'm so desperately sorry about it all.'

She was crying now, she couldn't help it. But somehow within minutes Josie was in bed, and Kyria Vassilou bathing her head in miraculously gentle fashion.

Then the local doctor was there, brought by Andreas, it seemed, to pronounce her likely to be laid up for some time, but in no danger, and to insist that David must have an X-ray examination just as soon as he could fix it up in hospital – adding optimistically that with up-to-the-minute treatment there was a chance that his shattered foot might be brought into better shape than before this last mishap.

There was little sleep for most of the grown-ups, at least, that night. Theo, now in a heavy slumber in his little room at the Hermes, had confided everything to David as clearly as he could on that grim pilgrimage home, and now David was taking a few minutes to repeat it to Mrs. Vassilou and Irene.

It seemed that from the moment Josie had caught sight of her aunt, that afternoon of her return from Troodos, all her old nightmare fears had rushed back. And later her aunt, by way of teasing her, as Irene had suspected she might, had frightened her badly. She had hinted that everyone at the Hermes would be relieved if she was taken back to London.

'Because Josie was scared, she started cheeking her aunt – telling her that she was a liar and a witch,' David said wearily. 'That's what I gathered from Theo, at least. And Mrs. Meredith was so furious she came out with something that made the child lose her head altogether. She wouldn't tell even Theo what it was.'

The door of the sitting-room and that of the girls' bedroom had been left open, and hearing a little wailing cry *'Yia-Yia'*,* Mrs Vassilou got up, and motioning to Irene to stay where she was, went up to the child.

For a minute or two David and Irene were silent. Then they heard Mrs. Vassilou's clear, thin voice raised in a little Greek lullaby, dear and familiar to anyone living in

* Greek (childish) – Granny.

Cyprus, and they both relaxed.

'Don't worry too much about our little Josie,' David said gently.

'I won't.' His words touched her, no less than his tone. 'I'm too thankful to have her home. But I haven't heard what happened yet.'

'She'd planned to hide up in the woods quite a long way behind the school,' he told her. 'Theo was to find a safe place for her and smuggle some food and picnic crockery there in stages. They took the things in the car, including the lilo, under Panos' unsuspecting nose, on different days. For a school picnic, Panos thought – not greatly interested, anyway.'

'And I hadn't a clue what was happening, either!' she exclaimed. 'Talk about conspirators!'

He grinned. 'They showed initiative, anyway. But to continue, Josie didn't mean Theo to join her in the hide-out. But when it came to the point he wouldn't leave her. Which was fortunate as it turned out.' He shifted in his chair, to ease his foot, which was clearly paining him. 'I abandoned the station-wagon very soon,' he went on, 'and went on searching for them on foot, shouting. I'd have given up much sooner and come back for some helpers, but here and there I found traces – a plastic cup, a scarf I recognized as Josie's – so I scrambled on. It was very rough, hilly ground and I was afraid they might have had an accident.'

'And they had, of course?'

He nodded.

'The sun had set by now, and suddenly Theo came running towards me, crying. They had lost the way to the cave they'd planned to sleep in, and while they were hunting around for the right direction in the half light Josie had missed her footing and crashed down to the bottom of a pretty deep and rocky gulley. She was lying there without moving. He thought she was dead.'

'The *poor* little boy!' Irene ejaculated.

'A very brave one, too. He'd got down to her somehow but couldn't make her speak or move, so clambered up

187

again to try to get help.'

'And you climbed down?'

'You could call it that. Though it was a quicker rate of progress than I intended. I managed to carry her up by a more roundabout way – took time, but it was worth it.'

'David, what a terrible ordeal for you!' She could hardly speak for distress, knowing what he must have suffered.

'It was sheer hell for the first moment, when I thought that Theo was right – that she was dead. In a way it seemed like history repeating itself. I was remembering the little girl I'd failed to save, years ago, in Glasgow. But when I realized that she was living and breathing – well, it did something to me, Irene, broke that haunting sense of failure. Oh, maybe you won't understand.'

'But I do, darling!' She couldn't have kept back the endearment if she had tried.

He glanced at her quickly, but before he could do more than exclaim: '*Irene!*' there was the sound of Mrs. Vassilou's descending footsteps and the next moment she had come into the room again.

'David,' she said earnestly, 'it's you Josie wants to see now. Indeed, lullabies and a sedative notwithstanding, she won't settle down until you go to her. But don't stay more than a minute or two.'

He went slowly upstairs, watched by the two women, pain shooting through his foot at every step, and limped into the bedroom. The only light came from the little lamp which Kyria Vassilou had left burning before the icon of the Virgin and Child. It showed Josie lying in a corner, and he went over to her at once.

She held out a small, weak hand, and whispered: 'Sorry, Uncle David. Very, very sorry!'

He bent over her. 'Darling little goose, don't fret any more, or get frightened over nothing. Even if Aunt Ethel had wanted to spirit you away, and she most certainly didn't, we wouldn't have let her.'

'She said everyone would be relieved. And when I said she was telling lies, she got just horrible, told me that